SNARED BY SABER

SHELLEY MUNRO

MUNRO PRESS

DEDICATION

For Paul, my husband, partner in crime, and fellow adventurer.
Every day is a good day.

INTRODUCTION

A capture gone awry might be the best mistake ever...

When a feline virus on Earth wipes out much of his race, Saber Mitchell moves his shifter family to the jungle planet of Tiraq. To provide an income—and keep the testosterone-fueled males from killing each other over the lack of mates—Saber opens Middlemarch Resort, specializing in women's capture fantasies. Unbeknownst to the women, some captures will be more permanent than others.

Saber has no plans to find a mate himself...until a capture goes awry, landing both him and "kidnapped" guest Eva Henry on the other side of the huge island. Saber must face birds, beasts, hungry natives and Eva's own penchant for escape to see her safely back to the resort.

Keeping his hands off her proves impossible...even after Saber learns mating Eva comes with bigger, more dangerous troubles than all their jungle perils combined.

Pronunciation Guide

Many of the alien characters within these pages bear Celtic names. Here is a guide to help pronounce their names:

Casey Seonaid: (kay + sea) shone + aid

Pryce Dearbhorgaill: (price) der + vor + gill

Almeda Dearbhorgaill: (elle + me + da) der + vor + gill

Loeiz Dearbhorgaill: (loo + eece) der + vor + gill

CHAPTER ONE

MIDDLEMARCH RESORT, IONE ISLAND, PLANET TIRAQ

"I shouldn't have come to Tiraq." Eva Henry plucked her communicator from her bag and glared at the round screen. *Nothing. Not a single* frying fungus *squawk.*

She shoved the red com-circle out of sight even as she prayed her assistant would call soon. She needed to know her careful plan was proceeding. "I should be back on Dalcon taking care of business."

"Wash your mouth with *crapola* soap!" Casey Seonaid, Eva's best friend, grabbed her forearm, her fingertips digging into Eva's flesh like scorp-pincers. "Forget work. This is your birthday treat. If anyone needs stress relief, it's you. Listen to Doctor Casey. Indulging in a capture fantasy is just the thing." Casey glanced around. "Where are we meant to check in?"

Eva forced herself to focus on the noisy chaos of dozens of women and their multitude of bags and let Casey drag her to the end of the line waiting for room allocation.

"Eva, take a gawk at his ass!" Her friend spoke in a reverent tone. "Wouldn't you like to take a bite? Or what about him?" Casey hummed a sexy sound and winked at her as a second bare-chested male strolled through the resort foyer. "I want a capture fantasy with *him*."

Her friend wasn't the only one to notice sex-on-legs saunter past. Eva observed the shy smiles, the blatant grins, heard the shrill whistle, the appreciative whispers about forced-sex fantasies at the men's hands. *Holy Finnian bats*, even *her* libido did a halfhearted jig. Something that had her stumbling mid-stride since she hadn't thought of men and sex since Pryce—

The cramped pain in her left hand jerked her from the tortured memories. Bloodless fingers gripped the handle of her bag, and she fought to regain her equilibrium, fought to get past the haze of red rage, fought to distance herself from the past until she trembled with the stress.

Luckily Casey didn't notice her zone-out, her friend's saucy commentary a steady rumbly purr of background noise. Casey continued murmuring and nudged Eva with a pointy elbow.

"Oh yeah. Hell yeah. This is right where we should be," Casey said, using her elbow again before Eva could evade. "My female parts are gonna get a good workout if those cuties are any indication of the resort merchandise. And about time too. A pox on the military and their *stoopid* fraternization rules. Capture fantasy, here I come!"

"Shush." Eva rubbed her ribs and sent a furtive glance at the other women waiting to check into the exclusive Middlemarch Resort on Ione Island.

Most female guests hailed from the nearby planet of Dalcon—the same as she and Casey—but they came from a cross-section of races. There were several blue-skinned Manx, some Labhras with their flickering skin colors indicating their fluctuating emotions, a powerful striped Tigrus, and a couple of compact Setanta with their distinctive straight violet-toned hair. Some came from races she hadn't seen before, and Eva didn't let her gaze settle into a stare. Unintended rudeness of that nature caused deaths every year, and she didn't intend to end up a statistic. Not now when she was so close.

Things to do.

Revenge to implement.

Despite herself, Eva slid another quick glance in the direction of two women whose heads were covered with swaying tendrils. Casey might recognize their race since she traveled a lot with the military.

"*Scurvy sky pirates,*" Casey said, suddenly breathless as she stared over Eva's shoulder. "I've changed my mind. I want one of *them* to capture me. No...no, all of them at once! I'm sure I could cope."

Eva caught a glimpse of tall, dark, and sexy seconds before her communicator gave a familiar squawk. She fumbled through the contents of her bag. Her hand closed around the com-circle, and she flicked it to active vocal. "Henry," she barked. "Tell me it's—"

Casey snatched the communicator, dropped it on the floor, and deliberately crushed it under the heel of her military-issue boot.

Eva gaped at the innards of her com-circle and took long secs to find her voice. "Why did you do that?"

"This is a holiday. For both of us. You work too hard and need a break, and I require recreation before I head to my next assignment. Please, Eva. I want us to enjoy ourselves. I won't see you again after I leave on assignment. Not for ages."

The forlorn note in Casey's voice made Eva look closer for the first time since they'd met up at the busy Dalcon spaceport. Were those tears shimmering in Casey's eyes? And she looked exhausted, with bags of fatigue beneath her lower lashes, as if she hadn't slept in days. Guilt flooded Eva. What kind of friend was she?

"I'm sorry. You're right." Her plans had taken eons to set in place. Several more solar days wouldn't make much difference. The result would be just as satisfying.

Vengeance for Pryce at last.

Eva hooked her arm through her friend's and urged her forward as the line wended its way to the reception desk. "Did you have a chance to make the new outfits you were talking about? Not that you'll spend much time in your clothes if you're captured as you wish."

"No." Casey's expression was closed off, and Eva sought a way to bring back the fun, smiling girl she'd met in the market many cycles ago, the young girl with the wild dark curls who'd towed her aunt from fabric stall to fabric stall and radiated excitement and enthusiasm as she stroked the shimmering materials of every color imaginable.

Now, not only did Casey appear exhausted, but she'd lost some of her bulk. Her wild curls were long gone, sheared off to leave brutally short fuzz. Something was dreadfully wrong with her friend.

Two men entered the foyer, both tall, dark-haired, with intense green gazes that crossed the roomful of gawking women with silent intent. They exchanged words, one nodding then replying.

Eva stared with everyone else. Sexy lips. Way too easy to imagine those luscious mouths roaming a feminine body, giving and taking pleasure.

"What about one of those two?" she whispered, using her chin to signal the direction. "Can you imagine one of them whisking you to the fantasy rooms? Forcing you to have sex with them? Or how about *them*," she said as three males joined the first two. Tall, all muscular with black hair of varying lengths, sparkling green eyes, and grins ranging from friendly to impish. "Do you think they're from a new range of bots? They're very alike."

To Eva's relief, Casey lifted her head, and her scowl dropped away. "Good choice." Her gaze lingered with feminine appreciation. "Bots or not, I hope we're chosen for the extras. Rumor says their fantasy rooms are the latest in new technology, and they cater to any sexual taste. They say the women have to be carried out because they're so drugged with pleasure. Then they're pampered in the beauty rooms with sensual massages and given the royalty treatment."

"Sounds exhausting." *Exactly what kind of extras?*

Casey gave a theatrical shiver. "You work hard. You deserve a little fun. Even if we don't get picked for the special captures, we'll get to partake in the other activities, have a fruity cocktail or three, some blistering-hot sex. Please, Eva. I want you to enjoy your birthday."

Eva flashed her friend a smile, hopefully a reassuring one, while she wondered what the special captures involved. Wasn't this role-playing and fantasies aided by technology? She was frightened to ask questions. "Don't worry. We'll have a blast."

The line shuffled forward, and the receptionist lifted her gaze, a professional smile pinned to her lips.

"Names, please." She was a pretty girl with green eyes. Her black hair was pulled back from her face and arranged in a tight bun on top of her head—a doughnut-shaped roll. She resembled the sexy males. They had to be bots.

"Eva Henry and Casey Seonaid," Casey said.

The woman's hands halted on her flat, glasslike keyboard. "Shone-aid?"

"Yes," Casey said. "But it's spelled S-e-o-n-a-i-d."

"Ah." The woman's hands flew over the keyboard, and she hummed approval. "Perfect, thank you for booking with the Middlemarch Resort," she said, sliding a genic mini-tab over the counter between them. "Your chalet number is twenty-five. There is a map plus information and instructions on the genic. Make sure you read them because missing crucial events or not following directives will lessen your chances of experiencing one of our special signature captures. Don't forget to attend the welcoming party tonight. Your luggage will be delivered, if it isn't in your chalet already. Any questions?"

Eva shook her head.

"I hope you enjoy your vacation at Middlemarch Resort."

Summarily dismissed, Eva gave the genic to Casey. "You're the expert navigator. You find our chalet, and I'll follow. What are the special captures? You haven't said."

"Nothing for you to worry about, I promise. We'll have a blast. Okay?"

"All right. I'll go with the flow and try to relax."

"Excellent." Casey sent her an approving nod. "Let's go."

Eva had seen luxury, certainly while attending functions with Pryce, but this place was impeccable, with stylish touches pulling everything together. The atmosphere oozed sensuality and good taste. Cream walls, arrangements of vivid fresh flowers, innovative lighting to spotlight erotic statuary. A water feature provided background noise. Top-of-the-line fixtures. They'd gone for classic styling rather than succumbing to technology streaming and the advertisements most hotels plastered over every available wall. Whoever the decorator was, Eva wanted to meet them so she could discuss refurbishing her restaurants to give her customers a more rounded dining experience. She followed Casey through a door and onto a gravel path.

The grounds were stunning, full of plants and fragrant blooms. A selection of variegated leafy bushes lined the path, their vivid blue and white flowers perfuming the air with exotic cookie spices. Tall trees with bright coral-colored trunks and green and coral foliage cast shade over the gravel walkways.

When they exited the trees, Eva caught her breath. "Oh, it's beautiful. I've heard...I mean, you told me planet Tiraq gets its jade-green color from the immense seas, and you've said how beautiful the water is, but I thought you were exaggerating."

The jade sea spread before them, the surface barely rippling. Already, women lazed on the beach of pristine white sand, and some from races that didn't mind getting wet were frolicking in the water. Eva couldn't wait to dip her fingers into the sparkling green liquid.

Casey gave a disdainful sniff and lifted her nose in the air. "This is our chalet."

Their chalet was the last in a row of carefully spaced accommodation. Thatched roofs kept out the weather and gave them a rustic charm. Beyond their chalet was a sturdy fence covered in fine mesh—the far boundary of the resort. Eva didn't mind since it would afford them more privacy than the chalets in the center of the resort. She might as well catch up on sleep while she was taking downtime.

"So it is. Looks pretty." Eva chuckled at her friend's put-upon expression. "Sorry. I'll never doubt you again."

"Then understand I crunched your com-circle for the greater good. I know you miss Pryce, but you can't mourn your husband forever. You're still young, and you deserve this holiday."

I don't deserve anything. Eva sucked up the swell of grief and put on her game expression. It slid across her face like an old friend, which told her how adept she'd become at pretense, at hiding the truth, at keeping secrets.

"Oh, look." Entranced, Eva crouched to pet a fluffy creature. Its black fur looked soft, while its big, round eyes emphasized the cute factor. "Come here, little fella. Casey, come see." Eva extended her hand.

"Don't touch it," a sharp male voice snapped.

Eva jerked her hand back even as the fluffy creature darted closer.

A huge black cat leaped in front of her, seized the creature in its maw, and bit down until the fluff ball stopped fighting. The cat flicked its tail and trotted off with its prize.

The man hauled her up by the arm, his green eyes full of alarm. "Did it bite you?" He grasped her hips and turned her to face him. Before she could answer, he ran his hands down her arms and legs. "Good," he said when he didn't find signs of any wounds. "The zylon didn't bite you."

"They bite?" Casey asked, looking dazed by the man and his sudden appearance. Not to mention the enormous black cat, which luckily had displayed more interest in the zylon.

"Yeah, their bite is poisonous, which is why we've fenced the resort to keep them out."

Poisonous? "There's a hole in your fence. I-I saw the-the creature crawl through," Eva stammered.

"We'll get it fixed," the man said. "I'm glad you weren't injured. That wouldn't be a good way to start your holiday. Let me get reception to send you refreshments to make up for the inconvenience." The man tucked Eva's hand on his arm and escorted her to the door of their chalet, where Casey waited. He disengaged and shunted them through the open door, then closed them inside.

"I don't think he was a bot," Eva murmured.

"The men here are sexier than in my wildest dreams," Casey said. "Bring on the captures, I say."

Eva's legs gave out, and she toppled onto the edge of a sleep-bed. She couldn't find the right brain cells to formulate an argument, let alone voice one. Hard to dispute the truth when it frisked you in such a delightful manner.

"What do you think?" Saber Mitchell studied his four brothers, who were currently crowding his office, two sprawled in chairs and the other two leaning against the walls. He scanned each of his brothers' faces before focusing on Felix, the second oldest of the Mitchell brothers. Leo came next in age, followed by the twins Sly and Joe. They had one more sibling, their sister Scarlett, who was the youngest of the Mitchell clan.

"I still think this is a crazy idea," Leo said. "Why can't we focus on farming the land? We had a successful farm on Earth. There's no reason we can't replicate that again."

"We don't need mates," Felix said, folding his arms across his chest. His green eyes—the same green eyes Saber saw in his bedroom mirror each day—offered a dare.

"They won't necessarily keep us on the straight and narrow," troublemaker Joe agreed. "Women are good for one thing."

"Your Mission Mate plan is flawed," Sly said, smirking at his twin. "Ma might think copying an idea our ancestors used successfully will fix everything, but it won't. I don't want to settle with one woman. Leo is right. We should focus on the land. If we're dog-tired, we won't have time or energy for fucking around."

Saber fought the urge to knock his brothers' heads together. No point wasting the energy. Violence wouldn't dent their heads or their confidence. Ever since they'd left Earth with a large contingent of friends and family to escape the feline virus, trouble had followed them. Often expensive trouble, with his brothers as the ringleaders.

"We don't have the luxury of waiting for the land to become productive." Saber strove for calm and logical arguments. "We have to take the assets we possess and use them to support our group. That means making the resort a success—and finding mates before the males kill each other."

"What about the zylon? Their numbers are increasing again. If they get through the protective fencing and into the resort, we'll have dead guests," Leo said. "Excellent publicity for Middlemarch Resort. It was lucky I grabbed that zylon this morning before the woman tried to stroke the bloody thing."

Saber failed to repress a shudder when he thought of the possible headlines that could race to Dalcon, their largest market so far. *Guests at Exclusive Middlemarch Resort Die from Zylon Bites.*

He couldn't let that happen.

"We'll go hunting tonight after the welcome party," Saber said, wishing he knew what was up with Leo. His normally even-tempered brother had become moody. He'd been acting weirdly since they'd left Dalcon. Maybe Ma knew. He'd ask at the next opportunity.

Saber drummed his fingers on the top of his desk. "You've all wandered through the foyer during check-in. Did any of the women catch your eye? Did you spot possibles for the first captures?"

"I went through the booking forms again last night. The two females in chalet twenty-five look good on paper," Felix said. "From what Scarlett dug up during her comp research, they have little or limited interaction with family. We could capture one of them."

"That was the two females Leo and I saw with the zylon," Saber said. "Did they book together? Do they know each other?"

"Scarlett said one of them booked on behalf of the other. I want a visual before I agree to go ahead. I'll deliver their luggage," Felix said and stood to leave. "If we don't like them after the capture, we can change our minds, right? They don't need to know the capture might become permanent?"

"You can change your mind if you don't gel with your capture." Saber hoped like hell that wouldn't happen. "Leo, you should check them out again. Help Felix with the delivery."

Leo muttered under his breath but pushed away from the wall and stomped after Felix.

"What's up with Leo?" Joe asked.

"I was hoping you knew," Saber said.

"We know nothing." Sly shot a mischievous glance at his twin. "Do you need us to do anything? I've got animals to feed, and the irrigation system is playing up again."

"No, that's fine. Just make sure you don't miss the welcome party," Saber warned. "And if the zylon population is increasing again, we need you both on the hunt tonight."

Joe flashed a cheeky grin and saluted. "Aye-aye, bro."

"We wouldn't miss the opening party for Mission Capture," Sly said, his expression a replica of his twin's— impudent.

Saber snorted and waved them out. He'd planned and schemed and lied to get to this point. The captures would work. They had to because he'd run out of options.

A tap sounded on his door, and he straightened from his slump. "Yeah?"

The door opened, and his mother, Anna Mitchell, walked in. She took a seat in front of his desk. "Everything set for the welcome reception? Can I do anything to help?"

His mother was tall and slender, her black hair long and without a hint of gray. She was the sole Mitchell without green eyes. He and his siblings took after their father in appearance. A widow of five years, his mother surprised most people when they learned she had six adult offspring. "No, Ma. We've planned for every possible contingency. I just pray this crazy plan works."

"It worked for our ancestors," she said, her gray eyes flinty with determination. "The original Saber Mitchell met Emily Scarlett at the first Middlemarch dance in New Zealand."

"But we intend to keep the women against their will. I don't think our ancestors went to that extreme."

Anna made a scoffing sound. "Females enjoy a man who takes control, one who protects them and makes them feel feminine. Every guest at the resort is dying to use the capture-fantasy room. Many of them fantasize about forced sex. We're providing a legitimate service, and the chosen women will be lucky to secure one of my gorgeous sons in return." She reached over and patted his hand. "Don't worry, son. Everything will work out for the best. It did for our ancestors. You only have to read Emily's diaries to know how happy she and Saber were together."

Saber prayed his mother was right. "Did Scarlett finish researching the Tigrus race? I want to know how compatible they'd be with us."

"She said she sent the last of the information you requested to your private mini-tab."

"Thanks."

Anna stood and glided to the door. "I'm going to mingle with the women and check everything is going smoothly."

Once again Saber stared at the closed door and hoped like hell this crazy plan went the way they hoped.

He slumped in his chair, exhausted—both mentally and physically. Tired of fighting for survival. Tired of looking after their people.

Just tired.

The welcome party was in full swing when Saber walked into the function room flanked by his brothers. His nostrils flared and quivered at the scent of lust thick in the air. His stride faltered as the wave hit him, reminding him he was a healthy feline male who hadn't had a woman for months.

Felix gave a soft whistle while Leo cursed under his breath.

"Everyone seems happy," Joe said in patent understatement. "Even Laurence is smiling for a change."

Music played, and several females were dancing with employees. Laughter and excited chatter battled the music, and some of the tension lifted from Saber's shoulders. Everyone looked happy. All the men they employed were talking or dancing with their guests. Doing their job, including Laurence, the brother of Saber's dead fiancée, which marked a change.

Taking care to keep his breaths shallow, Saber said in a low voice, "Go and check out the women on our list. Dance with them, speak with them, and come to a decision. We need to cement our plans."

As his brothers wandered off, Saber observed the partygoers. A flash of red caught his attention, and he turned to watch a woman progress to the bar. She wasn't exceptionally beautiful like some of the other women and was on the skinny side, yet something undefinable kept his gaze stitched in place. The red gown followed the lines of her body, its short length showcasing her legs and cupping her backside. Her footwear consisted of crisscrossed black straps and heels that elevated her height. She chatted with the bar staff, shared a smile with the other women who sat at the bar, and politely turned down a request to dance.

Interesting. He hadn't noticed any other woman saying no. Most were here to enjoy themselves and interact with the men.

Saber stalked closer, his mind taking in the small details and matching them against his brothers' tastes. Honey-blonde hair, swept into some complicated style that made a man think about messing it up. A slight, petite frame. Bright blue eyes, the color of the cornflowers his mother used to grow, swept over him, and dismissed him without pause.

Saber felt his mouth drop open and snapped it shut. Her rejection rankled. Miffed, he took a step toward her before common sense reasserted itself.

He wanted mates for his brothers.

He wanted them settled.

Happy.

This was business, and his own physical needs weren't paramount.

Saber changed direction and hit the far end of the bar. He

signaled for a drink and turned to survey the room before his gaze tracked back to the woman. Another female joined Blondie. Tall and regal with ruthlessly short black hair, she was dressed in a deep-blue dress with a dramatic slit up one side.

His attention shifted back to Blondie—just in time to see Felix swoop. Minutes later, Leo joined them and started chatting with the friend.

Saber watched for a few seconds longer, batted back the surge of inappropriate resentment, and decided everything was going well. He wasn't needed. His brothers knew what to do, and for once, they were following orders. He downed his drink and stopped to chat now and then, pulling out his rusty social skills to flirt and drag responding smiles from their female guests. Some of the women were stunning beauties, others not so much, yet their smiles and excitement, their enjoyment, made them all rate a second inspection.

He wove through the guests and employees, the lustful scents starting to get to him.

"Saber." His sister Scarlett waved him over to where she sat by the terrace doors.

He dropped onto a seat beside her. "What are you doing here?"

"I wanted to check out the guests, get a feeling for them." She delicately sniffed the air and grimaced. "Sucks to be a shifter sometimes." Her gaze drilled into him. "I didn't get to spend long on reception because you had me running background checks all day." She leaned closer, lowering her voice a fraction. "One of the women in chalet twenty-five doesn't have any family, although there was some scandal about her accusing her in-laws of murdering her husband. Nothing came of her allegations, and I haven't been able to discover anything recent on the subject."

"Pity we don't have time to visit her residence and ask questions in person. I worry we'll miss something important," Saber said. "What about the other one?"

"She comes from a military background, although sources say she doesn't spend her leave with her family. She seems closer to an aunt—her mother's sister. If we grabbed her, the military might become involved. The woman with no family might make things easier."

Saber tapped his fingers on his thigh. "True. Or maybe we should scoop up both women. If they both disappeared, we'd have some breathing space rather than leaving one behind who might cause problems and raise the alarm."

"Good point," Scarlett said. "We're treading a delicate line with our capture plan."

Low, throaty laughter came from a neighboring couple. It was sexy and suggestive, and the insinuation transmitted with ease. The resort employee stood and held out his hand to the woman, a Dalcon local, Saber thought.

"Care for a walk along the beach?" the man asked.

The laughter was a purr of response this time as she accepted his hand and stood.

Saber shot a glance at his sister. "You shouldn't be here, Scarlett. It's not right."

Scarlett reached over and rapped her fist against his skull. "Hello? Hello? Is anybody there?"

Saber ducked out of reach. "Cut it out."

"Then stop treating me like a kid. I know what sex is, Saber."

"Who told you about sex? Tell me so I can shoot their kneecaps."

"Saber!"

Saber grinned, silently acknowledging his sister was an adult. She wasn't a cute kid tagging after him anymore. "We're going hunting for zylon once this winds down. You wanna come?"

"You're on. Bet I catch more cute fluffies than you."

"You can try," Saber said.

Romantic cooing sounded outside, and Scarlett grimaced. "Ugh, I've seen enough. I'll see you later." She stood and sashayed

19

out the terrace doors. She paused to remove her shoes before stepping onto the sandy beach.

Saber watched his sister until she blended with the darkness. They had a couple of days to observe and decide. Maybe this capture scenario was bizarre and risky, but he was doing it for his family. Once they were settled, the burden of responsibility would lessen, and he wouldn't need to worry as much about his family's future. He could relax.

The door to the Dalcon restaurant burst open, the heavy wood crashing against the wall.

Robbie Campbell leaped to his feet, his cane clattering to the tiled floor. "Who—who are you? W-what do you want?"

"Where is she?"

Robbie gaped at the mountainous bald guy blocking the doorway. He stared at the broken door lock and back at the man. He swallowed. Hard. His heart stalled for an instant then battered his ribs like a captured wild creature attempting escape. "Who are y-you looking for?"

"Stand aside, man," a second voice said. A feminine voice.

The nanosecond Robbie heard her imperious order, he stiffened, cursing under his breath. This wouldn't end well.

The woman stalked into the empty restaurant. "Where is she?" she repeated, crisp and concise. Her voice didn't match her regal station or her high-class grooming. Her hard expression didn't go with the outfit either, and Robbie would bet the woman's titled Dalcon friends didn't often see this side of the Dearbhorgaill matriarch, not unless they landed on her shit list.

Like Eva, and by extension, him.

No point in trying to dodge questions. Mr. Brute would beat

the facts out of him. Hellfire, Lady Almeda Dearbhorgaill would order him beaten anyway—no matter what he did or said or how he begged.

"She went away for the weekend with her friend Casey. To some resort. It was a surprise for Eva's birthday so I don't know her location."

"I require her signature on some paperwork. When will she return?"

"Casey said they'd be away for five solar days."

Lady Dearbhorgaill scowled, then a crafty grin crawled across her features, and it was the scariest thing Robbie had seen since the day a bovinebeest charged him in the forest and injured his leg when he was a youth. Hellfire, he owed Eva his loyalty, but at what cost? What would the lady bitch do next?

"Call her."

Robbie hadn't managed to contact Eva since her com-circle cut out abruptly. He wasn't worried—much.

Robbie picked up his com-circle and pushed a button. Anticipating the next order, he put the unit on speaker so they could all hear the summoning tone. Robbie ended the call and stated the obvious. "She's not answering. Must be out of range."

"But I *need* that signature."

A trace of desperation echoed in the crisp notes, poking at Robbie's curiosity. Not that he was cracked enough to ask questions. Oh no. He kept his lips firmly closed, his gaze downcast to offer the respect the Dalcon elite expected from the lower castes.

"How are you paying the wages, the bills while she's away?"

"She left me several signed transfer certificates."

"I'll take them. Give them to me. All of them."

The wild creature in his chest took flight again, bashing the hell out of his ribs and attempting a new escape path up his throat. Gaze still downcast, he limped toward the small office at the back of the restaurant. His knees trembled, and for one horrid moment, he wondered if they'd fail and land him in a face plant on the floor.

Aware of the woman and the hulk at his back, he forced his legs to bear his weight and made it to the office. He sank to his knees, his hands sweaty and trembling when he turned the old-fashioned dial of the safe back and forth to the pre-set positions. He pushed down on the handle, and the multi-locks disengaged. Robbie's breath hissed out with relief. At least he hadn't messed that up.

He picked up the large envelope bearing the currency transfer certificates. They were blank and already signed by Eva.

"How many are there?" Lady Dearbhorgaill demanded.

"Th-three," Robbie said.

"Perfect." Her eyes glittered in a kind of sick triumph. "Ready cash?"

Robbie gulped. "Not much. Just a float for when we open. I-I've already been to the bank." Hellfire, he hoped the old bitch believed him.

"I'll take that too."

Robbie grabbed a faux-cotton bag and thrust it at the woman. She accepted it and shoved it inside her bag along with the envelope.

"Knock him out. Toss the place. Give the appearance of a robbery," she said and exited the restaurant without looking back.

No remorse.

No concern.

No guilt.

Just an uppity rich woman who thought she ruled the world.

Robbie blinked when the hulk lunged from his position. For a big dude, he moved fast. Robbie felt the rush of wind against his face seconds before the fist connected with his jaw. That was the last thing he remembered.

"Rob. Rob-bie." Someone was shaking the crap out of him. "Robbie, wake up."

Robbie groaned. His eyes flickered. Everything hurt. Especially his head.

"He's okay. He's alive," a female voice said. "Did ya call security?"

"On their way," a man said.

"What happened?" Robbie pushed himself into a sitting position. Nausea clawed its way up from his stomach, and he swallowed.

"Don't you remember?" Dina, one of the waitresses, crouched at his side.

"I..." He gazed around the restaurant, took in the toppled chairs and the wrecked tables. The lack of liquor bottles behind the bar. "Someone broke in."

"They've wrecked the place, taken food and booze. The safe is open," Dina said, her thin pixie face a shade paler than normal.

The clomp of boots had Robbie turning his head. The security men had arrived.

"What happened?" one of the uniformed men demanded.

"Someone burst through the door. They must've knocked me out. That's all I remember," Robbie said.

"Insurance paperwork's in order," a second security man said after pushing a few buttons and reading the screen of his genic mini-tab. "We can proceed. Take his statement while I question the neighboring traders."

Dina helped Robbie to his feet and righted a chair for him. He sank onto it. "Water," he gasped, and while Dina rushed to get water, his brain slipped back into gear.

Well hell. Eva had been right.

The stupid old bitch had taken the bait.

CHAPTER TWO

S omething woke Eva. An out-of-place noise. A faint rustle. A footfall?

She sat up in bed, eyes straining to pierce the darkness of their chalet. "Casey?"

Casey didn't answer.

"C-Casey?" Although she aimed for a firm timbre, her voice emerged coated with fear because her gut was screaming something was wrong. Casey was a light sleeper. Why wasn't she answering?

A prickling sensation crawled up her spine while her gaze roved the darkness, searching, searching, searching, as senses honed from growing up on the streets worked overtime.

Someone, *something* was in their chalet.

"Casey, are you there?" Her friend hadn't been sleeping well during the two solar days they'd been at the resort and sometimes went for a walk along the beach. Maybe that was it. She'd woken just as Casey was leaving. She listened for an instant longer and heard nothing. Slowly, she willed her body to relax, her breathing to return to normal.

A black shape leaped at her without warning. She screamed and scrambled back and away. A hand slapped over her mouth. Another pushed her flat to the mattress. Memories rose like a specter, tossed her into a thick pool of fear.

"Keep still. I'm not going to hurt you," a masculine voice growled against her ear.

Her breath seesawed in and out. A shudder went through her. He wasn't going to get her again. *He wasn't.*

She was stronger now. More capable.

She let her body go limp, waited for her captor to relax...

Then kicked, connecting with hard muscle.

"Fuck," he snarled and grabbed her roughly.

With a screech, she sank her teeth into his arm and bit down until blood flowed into her mouth. He bellowed, flinging her away. She was up and racing for the door before he could seize her again.

"*Oomph!*" She blundered into a low table, bashing her shins. The table skidded across the tiles, signaling her location.

Escape. She had to get to the door. Run to the next chalet for help. Find Casey. Frantic, Eva hugged the wall and slid toward the door, her gaze darting to and fro, trying to locate the man in the darkness.

He'd felt big, muscular but stalked like a predator, so silently. A tremble rippled through her body, her skin prickled, hair at the back of her neck lifted with foreboding.

Damn it. Where's Casey?

A hell of a time for her to do a moonlight flit.

Eva inched farther along the wall, trying to picture the chalet interior in her mind. She reached out, hit the door handle.

"Got you," a man whispered.

Eva yelped, and she ducked her head to bite again. Her captor

25

grunted, grasped her firmly, and tossed her back on the sleep-bed.

No surrender! No capitulation without a fight. She wielded her elbows, aiming for his ribs.

"Fuck it. Stop fighting." He cursed a colorful streak and snatched her again, fingers biting into her arms.

Strong. Too strong.

Gods, it was happening again...

"Let me go. Please, let me go, and I won't tell anyone." Her voice was scarcely recognizable, and she gulped, frantic for air. His hands shifted, grazed her breast. She lashed out with her fist, wriggled, kicked, sobbed. "No. No, no, *no!*"

"Fuck." The man's grip tightened, and he twisted what felt like rope around her wrists.

"No!" Panting, she lashed out with her feet. "Please don't do this." Terror crawled over her. Her pulse thundered in her ears. Fast. Choppy. She lashed out again and almost wriggled free. "No, let me go! Please, please. Don't hurt me!"

She backed up on the sleep-bed, toppled off the mattress, and hit the floor with a spine-jarring thump. Unable to break her fall, her head struck the tiles. Pain speared through her skull, stunning her for an instant.

He was on her in a trice, his weight pressing her down before she could gather her addled wits.

She felt a cloth pressed against her nose. Pungent and unpleasant, the scent brought tears to her eyes. Couldn't get away. Couldn't hold her breath. Stark panic loomed then, but it was too late. Had to breathe.

She slumped, edges of black sliding over her vision.

Lights out.

Nobody home.

"You done?" Saber's voice ripped through the darkness. His nostrils flared and he stiffened. "Who's bleeding?"

"She bit me," Felix said in an aggrieved tone.

Unexpectedly, a laugh escaped Saber. He flicked on the light and saw his brother sitting on the floor with the unconscious woman. She was bleeding too. "You hurt her. I told you not to hurt her!" For an unexpected second, Saber wanted to rip the scantily clad woman from his brother's arms, cradle her protectively in his own.

Sweet baby Jesus, he had to get past his...his...infatuation with this woman.

He didn't want another woman, didn't need one after Lori.

He clenched his hands into fists, the prick of claws bleeding through the tops of his fingertips shocking him even more. What the fuck?

"I didn't do anything. All I did was hold her so she wouldn't hurt *herself*. Why is she bleeding?" Felix asked in alarm upon seeing the woman's head. He brushed aside her blonde hair and probed the wound. "Honestly, I didn't hit her when she bit me. I heard a thump. She must've hit her head when she fell off the sleep-bed."

"Bring her. We'll treat her injuries on the way. Hurry before we attract attention." Saber waited until Felix picked up the woman and carried her from the room before he flicked off the light. He tried not to notice the generous swell of her breasts as Felix passed. He tried not to notice the length of her bare legs beneath the bit of pale-blue silk she was wearing.

He tried to focus on Lori, the woman he'd loved and lost.

He failed on all three counts.

"She's okay," Felix said when Saber joined him at the rear of the vehicle. "The bleeding has already stopped. I've sprayed the area with anti-infection serum." He strapped her into the vehicle's rear, checked her pulse, and nodded. "I'll stay with her, just to make sure the bleeding doesn't restart."

Saber gave a clipped nod and closed the rear door for his brother. He jogged around to the cockpit and strapped in, trying to get past his rush of guilt.

No choice.

Saber started the shuttle, and moments later, when they were clear of the resort, he hit vertical climb and punched in the coordinates for the camp. Instead of setting the vehicle to automatic pilot, he operated it manually, needing something to concentrate on besides his zigzagging thoughts. He'd failed Lori, but he wouldn't fail everyone else who depended on him.

By the time they reached the captive camp on the far boundary of their land, daylight had broken. Saber landed the vehicle and powered down. He opened his door and leaped out, the tweet and chirp of birds and insects an assault against his ears. The vivid flora on this island attracted bugs and beasties by the truckload. They seemed to thrive in the fragrant tropical heat.

Saber wiped the sweat from his forehead and strode to the rear of the vehicle. He hoped his family thrived too.

"How is she?" Saber's eyes went right to the woman, her pale face and her loose golden hair.

"Still sleeping due to the sedative on the medi-cloth," Felix said. "I'll wait around until she gains consciousness."

Leo appeared, with Joe and Sly trailing him.

Saber scowled. "How is the other woman?"

Leo lifted his hands in surrender. "Whatever the problem is—I didn't do it."

"Not guilty," Sly and Joe chorused.

Felix carried the woman past Saber. A low growl built in Saber's throat when he noticed Sly and Joe's undisguised interest, their gazes lingering on the woman's legs and breasts. The warning rumble escaped before he could halt it.

What was wrong with him today?

"Saber?" Leo asked.

Saber ignored his brother's prompting query. "She got hurt during the capture. How is the other one? Is she okay? Uninjured?"

"She's sleeping off the sedative. She might have a few bruises, but nothing worse than that."

Saber gave a stiff nod, his feline stirring uneasily under his skin. "I'm going for a run. Keep the women restrained until I return, even if they wake up." Saber unbuttoned his shirt and shucked his footwear and clothes. He pictured the black leopard and let the shift take him. Muscles twisted and reshaped, and he fell to all fours as black fur formed on his body. Fully shifted, his senses amplified. The bright colors jumped out at him while the earthy scent of the forest filled his lungs.

The camp was a small clearing with two rough huts to one side. After they'd sighted several zylon in the region, they'd built a sturdy fence covered with fine mesh to keep the wee beasties away from their captives. The last thing they needed was for their prospective mates to die of zylon poisoning. As it was, they were going to need to do some swift talking and romancing to get these two women to stay on the island, even though they'd signed up for a capture when they booked.

Edgy restlessness filled him, and he broke into a lope. It wouldn't hurt to check the perimeter and make sure they'd caught all the zylon during their last sweep. He exited the enclosure, scented the air, and allowed the pleasure of running to take over. The rush of cool air over his fur.

His sensitive nose discovered the scent trail of a zylon. A fresh one. Saber sped up and thundered through the vibrant yellow and blue undergrowth. Overhead, tall black trunks and branches and green and yellow foliage shaded him from the early heat of the sun-star. The scent grew stronger, and Saber slowed into stalking mode. His nostrils flared, his whiskers brushing delicately against leaves. Up ahead, he caught a flicker of movement in a large clearing. A zylon sniffed at a rock while another sprawled in the dappled sunlight.

Saber moved closer, quivering with the need to spring, to attack.

The zylon might look cute and fluffy, but he'd witnessed firsthand the agonizing death of one of his people when they'd first arrived on Ione. Luckily, they'd discovered bites suffered while they were in feline form didn't carry the same toxicity.

A shadow blotted out the sun-star, and Saber froze at the base of a black tree trunk. The zylon popped onto their hind legs, their alarmed chitter filling the clearing. A raucous cry sounded.

Before Saber could blink, a humongous bird dived down and plucked up one of the animals. The other zylon broke for cover and dodged to escape a second bird. Saber didn't move a muscle and watched, astonished, as the two birds rose and disappeared above the treetops.

Sweet baby Jesus. Why hadn't they seen those birds before?

Saber hastened into a lope and headed to the camp. Inside the compound, he shifted and pulled on his clothes. "Felix!"

His brother strode from the nearest hut. "Yeah?"

"I know why there aren't many zylon at this end of the island. I watched a bird catch one. A shit-ass big bird."

Felix chuckled. "Was it yellow?"

"No, it was— Very amusing," Saber said, remembering the vintage television shows they'd studied at school on Earth, what felt like a million years ago. One of them had a big yellow bird that talked. "How is the woman?"

Felix sobered. "I hurt her. I didn't mean to, but I hurt her. Saber, this is a stupid idea. Why don't we return the women to the resort and forget about the plan?"

"Fuck." Saber rubbed his hands over his face then shot a hard stare at Felix. "We need mates to stop the fighting between our males. Damn it, Felix. We're sitting on a testosterone powder keg, and it's going to blow if I don't find a way to keep women here permanently. We need the stability that women provide. You know that."

"Things have already been calmer since the first guests arrived,"

Felix said.

"But they're not going to stay. We need mates, children. Strong family bonds. We've found a place to settle, but we have to make it into a home. And we have to do this while ensuring the resort's a success because we're running low on money."

"Why the hell didn't you say something?"

"I didn't want to worry you all. We can't stop now, or we'll lose everything. I had to borrow money on Dalcon, the money we needed to get the resort running. I can't default on those loans. The trad-bankers weren't interested in financing me. I had to go to the market bankers. If the resort fails, if the males start fighting, our community will splinter. I *have* to keep us safe."

"Fuck," Felix said, his gaze losing some of its normal devilry. "Those market guys don't muck around."

"Which is why we have to stick with the plan now that we've committed our resources."

"You *still* should have told us how bad our situation was."

"Everyone has been working so hard. I wanted to encourage them." Saber caught a flash of movement from the corner of his eye. He turned and couldn't help a rueful grin. "Did you tie up your woman like I suggested?"

"No need. She was still unconscious," Felix said.

"She isn't now."

Felix turned in the direction Saber indicated. "Bloody hell. Where does she think she's going? We're in the middle of nowhere."

"She's a feisty one."

A familiar shadow blotted out the sun-star.

Saber cursed and started sprinting toward the woman.

Too late.

One of the big-ass birds swooped, talons extended, and plucked the woman off the ground.

Her terrified scream rippled through the clearing. Saber put on a burst of speed and jumped for the woman's legs. He gripped them, pulling with all his might, and for an instant, the bird wavered.

Then it flapped its mighty wings and rose into the air—taking the woman and Saber with it.

The woman screamed again and wriggled frantically. Saber didn't blame her. Horror skittered through him as the bird soared above the treetops, transporting them miles from the camp.

"Stop kicking!" Saber shouted above the whistle of the wind.

A treetop, higher than the others, tore at his boots, and he tried to tuck up into a ball.

The woman didn't halt her screaming but at least she ceased her kicking. Saber's arms ached from holding on, pain throbbing through his shoulders. Where the fuck was the bird taking them? A nest? Food for its chicks?

Saber tried to think, to plan.

The camp was no longer in sight. They'd flown over a vast ravine and the trio of volcanoes on the west side of the island was much closer now. A plume of smoke rose from one. Below, heavy forest covered the land, and to their right, a curving silver line indicated a river. Fuck, even if they managed to escape, they were miles away from the resort. Many days on foot.

Saber's arms quivered, his muscles screaming. He groaned.

"Let go," the woman yelled.

Saber groaned again, determined not to leave the woman alone.

A high-pitched shriek filled the air. Wind whistled past Saber's face. The woman screamed again, her cry full of terror. Saber twisted and cursed.

Another big-ass bird was heading directly for them—humongous talons outstretched and hunger in its yellow eyes.

CHAPTER THREE

E va dangled beneath the bird, clasped in its sharp claws. Dull
pinpricks of pain ached at her ribs while her legs burned
and felt as if they might break off at the hip sockets because
he—whoever he was—refused to let go. Fear scraped its way up her
throat as the second bird cawed a warning and headed straight for
them.

They were going to die.

Eva couldn't see any other way out of this mess.

The bird carrying them dived without warning, and the man
gripping her legs cursed as his legs dragged along the treetops. He
shouted, lost his grip on one of her legs as his limbs hooked in a tree.
A raw scream burned her own throat as panic had her struggling
fiercely.

The second bird soared after them, screeching a high-pitched
challenge. Talons extended, it dive-bombed. The first bird,

handicapped by their weight was slow to react, slow to maneuver. The collision between the two sent them all closer to the ground, and the man clutching her legs gave a horrid moan.

Fear worse than anything she'd experienced before seized her body, squeezed the breath from her lungs. An icy chill encased her. She was going to die.

The second bird came at them again. There was a horrid midair thud, and then they were falling, falling, falling.

Eva screamed, arms flailing to no effect. Air whooshed by, branches whacked and gouged her torso, and she hit the ground, the collision smacking the breath from her body.

Above them, the two birds continued their squabble. Eva was terrified to move, petrified to check to see if her limbs were intact.

"Lady, you all right? Can you move?"

"Eva," she said, gasping for breath. If she was going to die today, she wanted someone to know her name.

"Eva." Her name was a testy snap. An order. "We have to move in case the birds come back." He was closer now, his hands moving up and down her body.

She smacked them away but, goaded by his urgency, she attempted to crawl under a bush. A pained groan escaped.

"No, not here. Farther into the jungle where the trees are thicker." A shriek from overhead hardened his face. "Move. Now!"

Eva scuttled like a Dalcon mousekit trolling the market for rubbish. She practically dived into a bush, her pulse almost drowning out the strident calls of the birds circling overhead. Tremors racked her body until the flap of their huge wings and their *caw-caw* cries became distant.

Only then did Eva attempt to stand. Her muscles and limbs protested, but amazingly, she thought she was okay. Bumps and bruises. She'd be sore tomorrow, but it was nothing a little medical attention couldn't cure. She glanced around, took in the surrounding trees and plants. The island didn't look so picturesque after being dumped into the middle of the tangled, colorful wilderness.

In her peripheral vision, she watched the man stagger—the kidnapper who'd attempted to save her from the bird. What was his game? Did the Dearbhorgaill duo hire him? Either way, she couldn't trust him.

He gave a low curse and flung off his shirt. She gawked as he removed his footwear and finally found her voice when he yanked down his black trews.

"What are you doing?" she shrieked. "You have rocks in your head if you think I'm having sex with you."

"Did you just imply I'm crazy?"

"If the hat fits. I'm *not* having sex with you."

He paused again, his trews baring his hipbones, and shot her a cocky grin. It transformed his carved face into something mesmerizing. "I don't believe I asked."

Eva had to remind herself he was a kidnapper and not trustworthy.

The harsh shrieks of the birds flying overhead again had his expression returning to forbidding. The air seemed to shimmer around him, and right in front of her eyes, he transformed into a sleek black leopard.

Kidnapper, savior, kitty-cat. He just kept revealing layers, each more confusing than the last.

His eyes were jade green, the same color as the sea that washed the shores of Ione Island. She gaped, and something flew into her mouth. With a sound of disgust, she spat out the leggy bug and spluttered, wiping the back of her hand across her mouth. "Yuck. That was disgusting."

The big cat gave a bark that sounded disturbingly like laughter, and Eva glared at it. "Not funny, kitty-cat."

The cat's tail lashed back and forth, and its mouth opened to reveal sharp white teeth. A low growl emerged from the beast's throat. Eva took a step back, and the cat-man barked out another rough sound at her expense. Definitely amusement.

"Well, if you're so smart, how do we get out of here?" She attempted a shrug, and a sliver of pain shot down her shoulder. "*Ow.*"

The cat stared at her and, of course, didn't reply. Her skin tingled under the acute focus, and Eva scowled. She slapped at another bug, noticed the rips in her nightgown, the way her left boob was almost totally revealed. She tugged the fabric back into place, but the attempt was useless since the material had returned to its previous position.

All the while, those vivid green eyes never left her, but surprisingly, she didn't feel fear. Curiosity. Puzzlement. Yes. But if he'd intended to kill her, she figured he wouldn't have attempted to save her from the bird.

"Stop staring. It's rude. Besides, it's your fault I'm stuck in the middle of the forest in a ripped nightgown." Standing around wouldn't save her ass, and he obviously didn't intend to add to the conversation.

Eva glanced both ways, slapping at a red bug that landed on her bare arm. The forest appeared thinner to the right. While she could see the sense of sticking to the trees in case the birds returned, she'd end up covered in bites and scratched to pieces trying to force a path through the thick wall of plants. Better to take the easy way and keep checking for hovering birds.

Eva forced her aching muscles to action and headed to the right, picking her trail through the heavy undergrowth. She stumbled and limped over the rough terrain but at least it was progress. Way better than crying "woe is me" and waiting for rescue.

"Where the devil are you going?"

Eva halted and turned around. The cat-man had changed forms again and now stood in front of her. Naked. Every single striking inch of him. Her gaze hit his wide chest, bulky yet very touchable.

Unaccountably, heat rushed to her cheeks. He bore a mass of sculpted muscles on his tan upper body. The enticing definition extended down his torso, a muscular ladder tempting her to touch. Preferably with her mouth. Lower still, his hips were narrow, and his cock...

She blinked and ripped her gaze away.

"Enjoying the sights?" His gravelly voice held a hint of challenge.

A shiver zapped her, becoming a blaze as it shot south. Her mind went on a holiday—a byproduct of thumping to the ground. It had to be. That was the only explanation for her girlie reaction. It was all too easy to imagine him whispering in her ear, his hot breath misting across the whorls as he murmured sexual suggestions.

Whoa! She was getting way ahead of herself. But heck, his cock—it was growing before her eyes.

Flying Finnian bats.

His soft laugh jolted her, stopping her from toppling deeper into disturbing territory. She gasped, the sharp intake of air whistling through her teeth, and she jumped several paces away from temptation.

But her gaze continued to drift. She was looking at *it* again. No, touching would be plain stupid. There was a term for women who fell for their kidnappers.

He caught her staring again, chuckled louder, and the joyous sound reminded her of Pryce. Her husband had possessed a great laugh, one that invited everyone to join in with the joke.

No! Focus, you ludicrous lady lump. It didn't matter how pretty he was, how much she craved physical contact, or how her mind taunted her with the idea of having sex with him. He'd kidnapped her and was possibly on the payroll of the Dearbhorgaills because she couldn't believe *this* was what they'd meant when they'd mentioned special captures.

Casey had assured her that sex with one of the gorgeous resort employees would leave her relaxed, battle-ready, and in the perfect mindset to kick Lady Almeda Dearbhorgaill's ass. When she saw her friend again, she'd tell her she had been mistaken. Eva felt weak-willed and puny, and that was from only *thinking* about touching.

"I know how to use it." His words were a seductive whisper, implicit with promise. His dark brows rose, the tilt of his grin full of challenge. *Gamboling griffins*, one glance told her he'd be happy to demonstrate how his equipment worked.

"I'm sure you do." She aimed for dry and dismissive. "And maybe, if we were back at the resort in a nice comfy sleep-bed, I'd consider playing with you. But right now, every muscle in my body is screaming foul. I want a bath and clean clothes. Medi-serum on my cuts and scrapes. Then I'm gonna contact the authorities and press charges against the idiot who kidnapped me from my cozy room. Was it you?"

"Yes," he said without hesitation.

"For the love of St. Bridget, *why*?"

"You don't need to know that."

As she'd thought. He sounded cagey. The dastardly Dearbhorgaill duo hated her guts, hated her success, hated that she dared to remain in the same city and rub their aristocratic noses in her achievements. "I'll pay you more to let me go. I'm a wealthy woman. I can afford to double your fee. Besides, my friend will have raised the alarm by now. She'll be searching for me."

"We need to get moving. You're walking the wrong way. We need to go that way." He made a jerking motion with his thumb.

Eva had seen that expression before—one of male smugness and supreme confidence. She didn't waste her breath and turned away from him to limp in the direction she'd chosen. This was an island. She'd keep moving, maybe find a river or stream. Eventually she'd arrive at the coast, or maybe she'd come across a settlement where she'd offer payment to anyone who could get her off this island and away from the crazy cat-man.

Casey had said the island was a large one. A pity she hadn't bothered listening to the facts and figures her friend had spouted, but she'd been busy trying to sort out the menus and arrange staff to cover her absence.

She halted to ask, "How long will it take to get back to the resort?"

"It's a big island."

She flinched when a golden long-tailed animal shrieked and leaped from one tree branch to another in front of them. The creature seemed more curious than ferocious, and her pulse rate slowed from crazy fast to something resembling normal. She slid her gaze back to him. "But other people live here, right?"

"I haven't met them."

Something in his tone, his expression, sent a surge of fear through Eva. "Give me an estimate. A few hours to get to the resort?"

"Did you see the ravine we flew over?"

"I was too busy screaming." She needed to get back to Dalcon soon. A few solar days at most. "How long? A solar day?"

He shrugged and picked up his trews. *Hellfire harriers*, his ass was just as luscious as his front side. She tore her stare away and studied her toes. Much, much safer. She was finding it difficult to concentrate with the visual distraction. No doubt part of the Dearbhorgaills' plan.

"How long? *Tell me.*"

He avoided her gaze. "A good while, especially if we run into problems." He pulled on his clothes, cursed a little when he slid his feet into his boots. "Why do you think we should go this way? It's in the opposite direction from the resort."

"You said there's a ravine. The jungle looks thicker that way." She gestured. "There don't appear to be any paths, and we don't have tools. That reason enough for you, cat-man?"

"Saber."

"Good. Now I know the name of my kidnapper. Time's a wastin'." Eva limped down the path, the rocks and twigs on the ground hard on her bare feet. Her ribs ached, her legs felt weak, but she forced her limbs to move. She had to get off the island. It had taken long, long solar months to maneuver her in-laws toward her trap. This might be her one chance to expose them as liars and cheats.

Murderers.

Footsteps sounded behind her, the snap of a stick forcing a tiny *eek* of alarm from her throat. Her hand covered her thudding heart as she whirled to stare at him.

"Here, put these on. They might protect your feet. You can take my shirt too." He thrust the clothing at her, his features impassive.

Grateful, she accepted the shirt and pulled it over her head. She hopped on one foot and attempted to pull on the socks. Saber steadied her until her feet were covered, then stepped back, giving her space and a semblance of control. She eyed him with suspicion. "Thanks."

Kind of weird thanking a kidnapper, but good manners never hurt.

"Let me go first." Saber pushed past and strode in the direction she'd chosen. Eva stared after him, scowling. He slowed, glanced over his shoulder. "Are you coming?"

A raucous howl echoed in the distance, and Eva scurried to catch up. Going off alone in this wilderness didn't strike her as a good idea. She'd wait until they hit the coast or returned to the resort before unleashing her wrath. After that she'd head straight for the spaceport and resume her everyday life on Dalcon.

Sighing, Eva followed Saber through the jungle. She climbed over tree branches. She squeezed past bushes. She winced when sharp thorns clawed her bare legs. Periodically, the jungle canopy thinned before becoming dense again. Birds—small ones in jewel-bright colors—flitted through the treetops, their squawks ear-piercing as they squabbled over the fat red fruits growing high above their heads.

"How much farther?" Eva asked.

He sent her a withering look and kept walking, placing one foot in front of the other.

Eva had lost track of time since they'd been walking for hours. *Hours.* She thought of her in-laws, and with each step, her fury built. Her battle with them had started because Pryce had dared to do something of his own instead of coasting through life on his parents' expensive coattails. They'd viewed it as shameful, a slight, and after discouragement and admonishments hadn't worked, they'd rejected him.

Disowned him for trying to be his own man.

What sort of parent did that? Oh wait. Hers obviously weren't stellar either since they'd dumped her as a baby. But neither had they faked affection they hadn't felt. Her parents—in their own way—had at least been honest about their dislike for her. Pryce's parents still pretended they loved him, but Eva knew otherwise.

They'd paid an assassin to murder their son.

Tears—livid and painful—shrouded her sight and blurred the bright blue plants while the pain streaking up her legs with each stomp grounded her again, made her determined to see this battle through. Let them do their worst. Kidnappers. Assassins. Bah! They didn't scare her. She'd get her revenge even if she had to return in an incorporeal form to wreak havoc in their luxurious mansion on Titled Hill.

Light streamed through the canopy ahead, and she blinked until her eyes became used to the brightness. At least picking her way along the almost nonexistent path was easier than trudging through the full jungle. Unfortunately, it also gave her a better view of Saber's ass.

Her foot caught on a concealed stick, and she cursed, furious at herself for not watching where she was going.

Kidnapper. Kidnapper. *Kidnapper!*

She picked herself up and continued trudging after that tight, muscular ass. She'd pretend it was one of those teaser-treats they'd started using in the hell-horse races—an incentive to get the hell-horses moving and racing each other.

A crash sounded in the distance, the echo rolling across the sky and vibrating through the ground beneath her feet. She came to an abrupt halt, eyes scanning the sky. What the heck was that? Another creature? A mythical dragon?

The thunderous noise repeated again, much closer now. A bright flash of light lit the pink sky with flashes of deep rose and scarlet.

"Rain," Saber said. "We need to find shelter."

"That's thunder?"

"Yep."

Drops of rain started to beat down on the leaves, bouncing off to strike her limbs. Steam sizzled from the hot ground, making the air thick and hard to breathe.

Saber grasped her forearm and propelled her under the shelter of a tree.

She dug in her heels. "Isn't it dangerous to stand under trees during a storm?" She had a vague recollection of some expert on the vids going on about safety during solar and land storms.

"You want to waltz out into a clearing where the birds might spot us, then you go right ahead."

"If they were smart birds, they'd go to their nests or wherever they hang out and keep dry," Eva snapped.

Saber's fingers bit into her upper arm, forced her to move. The rain made everything slippery and the footing treacherous.

"Stop rushing me." This was a nightmare, a bad dream, and she'd wake up soon. Everything would be back to normal. She'd be back in her flagship restaurant, training a new chef and steering clear of her in-laws.

"Have you thought about other animals? Predators? Did you notice the prints along the way? The broken branches?"

Holy Finnian bats. "Predators," she whispered, the word torn away in the splatter of the rain against the leaves. "I was born in the city, lived there my entire life," Eva raised her voice, her tone a smidge above freezing point. "I know city things. If I'd wanted to traipse around the jungle wearing socks and a shirt, I'd have made sure to include a scary-animal training course in my repertoire."

The loud crashes continued overhead. The sky darkened to a deep crimson, and water started spilling from the sky in hard, icy drops. The clammy humidity dissipated, replaced by cold and wet. The water seeped through her socks, shirt, and the remnants of her expensive nightgown. It drenched her hair until every lock plastered against her scalp.

Saber kept walking and she traipsed after him, each step an exercise in torment. He stopped without warning, and she plowed into the back of him. His body was as hard as a rock.

"Ow," she muttered. "What now?"

He pointed at a rocky face, which had an opening. "Shelter," he said. "We can wait out the rest of the storm in there."

"What if there's already an occupant?"

"Then we'll square off, and the winner will take possession."

"Ha-ha," Eva said.

"Wait here."

Eva opened her mouth to argue then snapped it shut. If he wanted to act the hero, let him. She sank to the ground, more exhausted than she'd ever felt after working a full day at one of the restaurants.

A touch on her shoulder shot fear through her. She scrambled back, throwing up her arms in a defensive manner.

"Steady," Saber said. "It's me. The cave's clear. We can shelter in there."

Eva clambered to her feet with a tired nod and limped after

the sure-footed Saber. The cave held a gamey scent, and her steps faltered. Her nose wrinkled, and she adjusted her breathing, taking in air through her mouth. "Are you sure it's safe in here? What if the owner returns?"

"The scent is a few weeks old."

"I'm glad I wasn't here with the beastie then. It must've really stunk." Eva sank to the ground again, shoulders slumped as she peered outside. The rain was so heavy there were already tiny rivulets of water rushing to fill dips in the ground.

The thud of a boot against rock jerked her head around. Saber was busy taking off his footwear. She didn't say anything until he peeled out of his trews.

Her hands slapped across her eyes. "What are you doing?"

CHAPTER FOUR

E va Henry was a curious mixture of brave and smart, practical and quirky. She tempted him, made him ponder the sensuality shimmering beneath her protective shell.

Saber grinned, saw her arrested look as she peeked through spread fingers, and his mouth widened to a full-out smile.

"What are you doing?" she repeated and raised her chin.

"You're beginning to sound like one of those squawky birds." At least he'd managed to contact the resort. He'd worried his com wouldn't work way out here, but now Felix knew not to worry or bother sending out search parties. And as it turned out, his brother was happy Saber had flown off with Eva because he already had his eye on someone else.

A chuckle escaped. Felix was keeping things close, not saying much, but Saber had heard his brother's happiness. His plan was working.

"Very funny. I told you I'm not interested in sex."

"What makes you think *I* am? And you came to a resort that caters to feminine fantasies. How does that work?" Felix told him that Eva hadn't entered the reality suites or paired up with any of the male employees. That pleased him.

She snorted. "*All* men are interested in sex."

It was his turn to grunt. "You might as well tell me. We have plenty of time."

She aimed a glare at him. "I don't want to chitchat. I want to go home."

Saber finished peeling off his wet trousers and hung them on a rock. She watched him the entire time with a half-fascinated, half-wary expression that tickled his funny bone. "You should take off your clothes too."

"No."

"It was a suggestion for your benefit," he said. "But if you want to freeze that's fine with me." Saber found a place to settle near her, facing the entrance in case any beast decided to wander into the cave. He found his gaze continually drawn to the woman. She'd started to shiver, and he hated to see her suffer.

"Tell me about the resort," she said. "Who owns the place?"

"My family," Saber said.

"A family-run fantasy resort? Sounds a little odd."

Saber hesitated, then went with gut instinct. They might be misrepresenting the resort to a handful of women, but he'd give Eva as much honesty as possible. "I won the resort in a poker game on Dalcon. The place was run-down. Not worth much. We needed a home and decided to check it out. My mother was the first one to see the possibilities and we went from there," Saber said, navigating between truth and reality.

She cocked her head, and even in the dim light, her expression blazed with curiosity. "How big is your family? Won't they be worried about you?"

"Of course they will. Felix—he's the oldest brother after me—will organize a search party. We won't be out here long." *Just long enough to engage your interest.*

"I saw you when I first arrived at the resort. You were with a group of men."

"My brothers. I have four brothers and one sister. Felix, Leo, Sly, Joe, and Scarlett. My mother keeps the family records, and we're all named after ancestors."

"From?"

"Earth. We came from a country town called Middlemarch in the South Island of New Zealand."

"Earth? That's a long way from Tiraq."

Saber shrugged, not offering more. Her shivers increased to short, sharp vibrations that rippled through her delicate frame. The woman, with her slight build and blonde hair, couldn't be more different from Lori if she tried. Her serious air. The way she lifted her chin in silent challenge.

"Did you know shifters have a higher body temperature? I could get you warm again."

She shot him a suspicious look. "How often does that line work for you?"

"No line. Feel my arm." He held it out and waited. "Ah, well. If you want to chatter your teeth all night, it's none of my affair."

"The rain will stop soon. We'll be able to walk until dark."

"Once the rain comes, it sets in for the afternoon. It won't stop before nightfall."

"But it might."

"You're welcome to go out on your own. Of course, we don't know what type of animals might be lurking in the forest. There could be more birds."

"You're trying to scare me."

Saber wanted to smile even though the expression was pretty foreign to him. Hell, he'd smiled more today than he had since leaving Earth. "Is it working?"

"I-I hope I never come face-to-face with those birds again."

"Me too."

She met his gaze for an instant before looking away. Another shiver worked through her. Saber didn't know if it was from the cold or the remembered terror of the bird seizing them. Before he even knew what he was doing, he was reaching for her.

Fuck, she was freezing.

He stripped off her socks. "I'm going to take off the shirt. Give it a chance to dry," he said.

Her gaze was wary as she trembled harder. "I'm so cold."

"I know, kitten. Let me get you warm again." When she didn't argue, he pulled up the wet shirt and tugged it over her head. The nightgown came with it. He arranged the garments over a large rock and settled on the ground with her soft weight atop him, in his arms. She cuddled against him, her nipples hard, cold points poking his chest.

Gradually the chill dispersed from her body along with the tension in her muscles. Her breathing became softer, and Saber smiled against her hair. Given time she'd become used to him, learn to trust him. She'd make him a good mate, and in return, he'd give her a secure home, friendship, and loyalty. Maybe they'd even come to love each other.

The thought gave him pause. No. He didn't want love, didn't want to make himself vulnerable in that way again. When Lori had died, it had almost killed him. Only his family's need for him had forced him to keep going, to step into his current leadership role.

He lightly stroked her body. She needed more flesh on her bones but fit against him perfectly. Yeah, they'd fall into friendship, and that would be enough.

Eva woke feeling warm and toasty. The pillow beneath her head was firm, while her surroundings were a true black, which nothing pierced. Where the *jumping jackabee jitters* was she?

The hard surface beneath her head moved. A hand moved down her back and settled on her bare bottom. Her breath caught halfway up her throat while she sprinted through her memory files. Holiday. Resort. Big freakin' bird. Cat-man. Rain. Cold. Toasty warm...

The hand on her backside lingered, heat emanating from the palm pressed against her tender skin. The warmth flowed into her body. Her skin tingled while her female parts, her pussy... Eva bit back a sudden urge to cackle. Cat-man. Pussy. They certainly went together. Maybe it was a sign.

A tiny snort escaped her, and the arm around her back tightened momentarily. "You're awake."

She could hardly pretend otherwise now that she'd revealed her alertness. "What time is it?"

"Not long until solar rise." His warm breath whispered across her cheek and added another degree to the fever burning beneath her skin. It had been so long since someone held her, comforted, and protected her without expecting something in return. And if she hadn't met Pryce, she'd never have known what she was missing. The burst of guilt dissipated some of her ease. She stiffened.

"I'm not going to hurt you. It wouldn't be good for resort business if reports surfaced that we abuse our customers."

"But you'd kidnap them," she retorted.

"In fairness, we catnapped you," he said. "A fine distinction, to be sure, but we should get the facts right."

Eva sputtered and the sound was a close cousin to humor. This...man, she decided, didn't behave like the males in the market where she'd grown up. He didn't behave like the customers in her restaurant. He had a weird sense of honor. She gave a mental shrug, unable to get a handle on Saber.

The hand on her buttocks shifted, and she almost let out a sound of complaint. *Holy Finnian bats*. What was wrong with her? She had to move away.

Yeah, she'd move any second now.

His hand resettled on her back and smoothed down her spine in an exquisitely slow journey before it came to a halt on her butt again. For long seconds, his palm warmed her skin before he lifted it again to repeat the process. *Frying fungus*, that felt so good. She wanted to arch beneath his touch and encourage him to press harder, to go faster.

A low chuckle, not far from her ear, made her freeze.

"I'm not going to hurt you."

Eva became aware of something else, something other than the hardness of his chest. Tension bolted through her muscles, and the hand stroking her came to a halt on her butt cheeks.

"Ah, you've noticed," he said in a cheerful tone.

"Difficult not to when it's poking into me."

"Yet you haven't moved." The whisper held a note of taunting. Maybe a hint of a dare.

Fear and disappointment coiled her guts into a tight knot. "If you intend to rape me, you'd better get started. I want to get moving."

"Eva. Kitten." Strong arms lifted her and held her away from the steely erection that burned her skin like a hot poker. "I do not, nor will I ever, force myself on women." He spoke slowly, and his words contained an underpinning of pissed. "For some reason, women adore my green eyes and my muscles. I *do* have a brain, but they don't seem to appreciate that nearly as much as my sexy body."

A snort escaped Eva before her mind had the chance to censor. *Humor. React.* The thought sprinted from her brain to settle on her lips in a grin. She found herself relaxing, and after a long moment, he pressed her against his body again. He was so warm, and Eva melted into his comfort with relief. It was even better when he placed his hand on her back and resumed his casual petting.

"Of course, that doesn't mean I'm averse to the idea of fucking you. You're soft, and your skin is like silk. I bet your pussy would feel perfect around my cock."

A flush swarmed over her body and converged at her breasts and the spot between her legs that had ached insistently since she'd first woken in his arms. "Are you always so...so...direct in your communications with women?"

He chuckled. "I enjoy fucking a woman's mind as well as her body. A little dirty talk works for me. Twice the pleasure."

"Oh." *Holy Finnian bats.*

"The moment you give consent, I'm going to suck those pretty tits into my mouth. I'm going to suck hard until you feel it right here..." His fingers drifted low on her buttocks to where her thighs and ass met, and he cupped her warmth. "I'm going to finger your pussy, and when you're squirming with need and panting with pleasure, I'll stick my cock inside you. I'll shove deep and give you the best fuck I can. Once we're finished, you'll feel as if you've been possessed, you'll have screamed in pleasure—and you'll beg me to do it all over again."

Eva sucked in a huge breath, more turned-on than she could ever recall. Those damn tingles were back, now *all* over her torso, her arms, her legs. *Frying fungus*, her body voted for his plan.

"You came to the resort to relax," he said, the rough gravel in his voice stirring nerve endings the length of her traitorous body. "I know we're in the middle of the jungle, but I'm happy to fuck you. At the resort, you'd only have the reality room."

His implication brought another twist of humor to her lips. The man had a healthy ego, implying he was better.

Eva lifted her head and tried to discern his face, but the darkness of the cave foiled her sight. She resettled against his chest. "Prove it," she said.

"You've told me—very insistently, I might add—you're not interested in sex. And now you're daring me to prove my prowess?"

"You've made several claims." Eva licked her lips and found that damn grin had set up shop again. "I'm suggesting you prove you can do everything you claim. I bet other women just accept your boasts." Eva drilled a finger into the middle of his muscular chest. "I have to experience your claims myself before I can believe. Proof."

Eva bit her bottom lip as silence fell between them. She wondered if she'd pushed too hard, punctured his masculine ego beyond repair.

Without warning, Saber slid her body upward, his tongue playing with the tip of one breast, tracing patterns around the areola until her nipple became an achy peak. Unhurried, he played with her breasts until she wanted to protest. He hadn't said anything about slow. In fact, she'd expected he was all brag, and he'd turn into a two, maybe three-second wonder. Shove it in and pull it out, ready to get on with his day.

Chagrin belted her over the head even as she finished the thought.

Saber chose to move to the next step on his agenda. He sucked one nipple deep into his mouth, pulling strongly until her body communicated its pleasure, every nerve ending standing to salute.

She groaned, felt the surge of wetness between her thighs. "Don't stop. Please don't stop."

A hard thigh chafed her pussy, and she found herself squirming against the resistance, rubbing against him to release the tightly wound tension creating havoc with her mind and body.

"Saber, please. Please. I need...I need..." *Frying fungus*, she needed his hard cock, the one that had made her cautious because she *knew* men, had experience that warranted such wariness.

This. Saber. He made her feel quite different emotions.

He released her nipple and she felt bereft. A pained groan of protest whispered past her lips.

"Tell me what you need, Eva."

"You." Gods help her, but she needed him.

"How do you need me? Tell me what you want me to do."

Eva bit her lip. No one had ever asked her that before. They'd always taken...even Pryce. She stiffened, and a flashflood of guilt roared on the heels of this betrayal.

Saber licked her other nipple, lightly bit it, but didn't suck with the intensity of earlier. "You have to tell me, Eva. I can't read your mind."

Lucky for her. She'd die of mortification if anyone else saw the inside of her head, listened to her innermost thoughts.

"Eva." The quiet insistence in his tone told her he wouldn't budge from his stance.

"I want you to suck my other breast." Suddenly, she was glad of the lack of lighting. He wouldn't see the blaze of embarrassment coloring her cheeks. "And maybe you could touch me down there too."

He barked out a laugh, sharp with a hint of rust, as if he hadn't had much to laugh about recently. "You want me to suck your breast and tickle your feet?"

"No!" The word came out in an explosion of air. "I want you to touch my pussy, finger my clit and stick your cock inside me. I want you to fuck me and make this edgy feeling go away. It's only fair since you started it."

"I can do that." A definite growl.

He sucked her breast, and she felt his sharp teeth marking her flesh. If anything, it made her hotter, more desperate for him to fill the empty ache that was driving her insane. His hands wandered her body, leaving heat and tingles in their wake. She jumped a little when fingers slipped between her legs and slid across her wet folds.

Eva shuddered. *Gamboling griffins*, he excelled at this sex stuff. Maybe it wouldn't hurt when he shoved his thing inside her.

His fingers strummed her, and he seemed to know the right spot to touch to ratchet up the achy need. He released her nipple and lifted her body until she sat astride him.

"Lift up. Take me inside you."

An order. A helpful order because she'd never done it this way before. Of course, living in the market, she'd seen sex in all its forms, but the actual *doing* was different from a visual. Awkwardly, she rose on her knees then grasped his cock in her hands. He was hard and hot and much larger than she recalled.

She fumbled, half expected harsh words or a quick slap.

When neither scenario occurred, she gave in to her curiosity and stroked his cock. She explored the hard length of him from tip to root. A rumble sounded, and she halted her petting.

"Keep going," he ordered.

She repeated the move, discovered a bead of moisture on his tip. The rumble reoccurred, and she realized it was a purr—his way of indicating pleasure.

"Put me inside you."

Eva directed his cock to her entrance and sank down. His flesh pierced her an inch at a time, filling the gnawing ache and replacing it with another one as he stretched her to the point of pain. His large hands spanned her hips, lifted her body a fraction then filled her a little more. He raised her again and forced her down, driving deeper into her flesh. The sensation wasn't as uncomfortable as she'd expected, and after several slow repeats, he filled her balls-deep.

"Eva," he whispered.

When she looked in his direction, she found the cave had lightened slightly. She could see the outline of his face, the flash of sharp white teeth. "Yes?"

"Start moving, kitten. Up and down. Take what you want."

"I thought you were going to fuck me?"

He chuckled, and she found her lips curving into a smile. "I can't do that on this stone floor. I'd rub a layer of skin off your back. Wait until later today."

"A shower and a soft sleep-bed."

"Exactly," he said after a brief pause. "My hide is tougher than yours. Do your worst."

Eva rose and sank, taking him back inside to the root. She paused, sighed. Although he filled her to the point of pain, it registered on the good side. She lifted, felt his hands band her hips again, and guided her into a faster pace. Threads of pleasure chased from her core, raced across her skin. She'd felt the same phantoms before with Pryce, knew they'd lead nowhere, but she was determined to enjoy them while they skated through her body.

"Wriggle around to get the right angle," Saber said. "Touch yourself. It makes me hot when a woman goes after her pleasure. Knows what she wants."

Eva frowned, felt her brow crease in an echo of her mouth. She wanted to follow the phantoms. She lifted up, still guided by his hands at her hips, flexed her hips, and changed the tilt of her body.

This time his cock touched a sensitive place deep inside her body. She groaned and repeated the motion. *Flying friggin' Finnian bats*!

Saber shuddered, and the shiver reverberated through her, hitting that sweet spot deep inside. Her fingers slid down to trace over the base of his cock. Her knuckle scraped across her hot flesh and a spasm shot through her sex. She tightened around Saber's cock. A tendril of pleasure streaked down her legs to her toes and filled her with exhilaration.

She lifted and slammed down, combining the move with the glide of her fingers over her damp flesh. The musky scent of sex filled the air, while the sounds of fucking brought heat to her cheeks. She repeated the quick shove, the prickles of heat and phantom feelings solidifying into a mass of painful pleasure.

Hellfire and poxy whores. She didn't know whether to stop because it hurt or keep going in case it got better.

Saber took the decision from her, his hips thrusting upward repeatedly, his cock filling her with brutal intent. The painful pressure intensified then exploded without warning.

Eva cried out as Saber plunged into her hard and fast, man-grunts echoing off the cave walls while her flesh rippled around his shaft, the spasms going on for long pleasurable seconds before trailing off. Saber stilled, his hands bruising her hips, his head thrown back, and his eyes firmly closed.

Eva let her gaze run over the savage beauty of his face and couldn't regret giving in to his sexual allure. She'd never felt this relaxed before.

Saber released his grip and tugged her down until she sprawled on his chest. Their bodies were still connected, but Eva couldn't summon the energy to move. Not even thoughts of his sexual history, the vague curiosity about where he'd learned his skillful ways, plagued her mind, which was surprising. The possibility of disease or pregnancy wasn't a worry either since every woman visiting the resort was required to have medical shots and produce a certificate to prove their clean bill of health.

No, she could return to Dalcon secure in the knowledge that only memories—good memories—would chase her from this casual liaison.

"It's lighter out. We should think about moving," Saber said, loath to move but knowing they should.

"I guess." Eva's stomach complained in a thunderous rumble. Embarrassing enough to heat her cheeks. "What are the chances of finding something to eat?"

Saber hid his amusement. "Think positive. We're bound to find edible fruit on the trees." He'd seen the odd fruit tree yesterday, but wildlife had stripped them of their bounty. "I'm starving."

"What's your favorite food?"

"I enjoy a good juicy steak on the rare side." A shifter's favorite food involved anything with meat. She'd learn that soon enough.

"What do you eat with the steak?"

"I prefer my steak to cover the plate, which doesn't leave room for green stuff. My mother says our ancestors ate vegetables with their meat. She says if it's good enough for them, we should follow suit." And he recalled the arguments around the dinner table. Vegetables first then the meat. Happier times. Easier times. Times before the virus had broken families, broken dreams, broken the future.

Killed Lori.

He must've made a sound because Eva lifted her head to stare at him. Her blue eyes looked sleepy and satiated, which pushed a bolt of satisfaction through him. He'd pleased her and released the cork on his own sexual frustration. Fuck, she'd almost blown his brains clear of his skull with her throaty cries and sexy shudders.

"Are you afraid of your mother?"

It took long moments for him to realize she was speaking to him, waiting for his reply. "Of course not. I respect her. She and my father didn't have much money when they married, yet my brothers, sister and I never lacked for anything. We had an idyllic childhood."

"My parents discarded me in the Dalcon market."

The hard note in her voice told him the act had scarred her and she didn't forgive easy, not that their actions were defensible. Fuck, what kind of parents did that to their child—left them like a piece of rubbish?

"Do you know who they were?"

"No, but only whores and thieves frequent the marketplace and the surrounding slums during the night. Decent folks—the traders—come out during the solar hours."

Saber's breath caught, but her stony expression told him not to pry despite his myriad questions. "I'm sorry. That can't have been an easy childhood."

She was a mixture of contrasts, and he wondered how she'd managed to stay so...untarnished.

Innocent. Yeah, that was the word he wanted. She didn't look as if her hard life had sucked the juice from her. His mind skirted the fringes of the horrors that would have greeted her on a daily basis—a life very different from his childhood and the fun and freedom he'd enjoyed. Lazy days of fishing with his brothers and cousins, having the run of the countryside, rushing in and out of friends' houses while his parents worked.

He wanted to ask more questions, but her rigid shoulders and tight lips didn't encourage his pursuit of the subject. He knew quite a bit about her but wanted to hear everything from *her* lips. "What do you do on Dalcon?"

"I run two successful restaurants and want to expand." Her chin lifted in a show of pride.

"So you're a good cook?"

She nodded. "I can do anything relating to the restaurant. Cook, clean, and serve customers. Everything."

"A boss should know how to do the tasks he asks his employees to perform."

"Exactly."

Her sharp reply held approval, and it made him want to smile. Despite himself, despite his remorse over Lori's death, he wanted to please Eva. Would spend his life trying to please her if he could, but he wasn't stupid enough to tell her that. Now was the time to hook her attention and play that line until she surrendered. He had privacy and few distractions. The completion of the task was up to him.

"Let's go." Saber eased her to his side, then stood and extended a hand.

She winced as she straightened.

"You all right?"

"Sore muscles." She glanced down her body, seemed to catalog her aches and pains. "I'm bruised."

Saber inched closer. "You want me to kiss them better?"

"I need medi-serum. I'll get some at the resort. It can't be as far away as you think."

"Let me see."

He reached for her, but she slipped from his grasp. "Bruises won't kill me."

Strong. Self-reliant. Smart.

Saber mentally cataloged everything he'd learned about Eva. She was the type of woman they needed for their clan—a worthy woman.

His woman.

CHAPTER FIVE

E va paused at the mouth of the cave, scanned left and right then looked up through the gaps in the canopy. Hopefully her clothes, or at least Saber's shirt, would dry better now than they had in the cave because, at present, the fabric clung with uncomfortable clamminess. The blue nightgown she'd discarded as next to useless.

She took two steps down a narrow path before strong fingers banded her upper arm and dragged her to a stop.

"I'll go first." Saber brushed past her and took point.

"Why?"

Saber halted and gestured with his hand. "By all means. Take the lead, so I can watch your ass jiggle."

Eva stalked past and tried not to touch the infuriating man. She didn't have a jiggly part on her body. In fact, Pryce used to tease her and tell her to eat more, which reminded her she was hungry.

Her stomach gurgled in confirmation, and she increased her pace, trying to forget about the hulky cat-man who padded behind her.

Soon she became aware of another urgent need.

"I need to...need to..."

"Go behind the bushes over there." Saber pointed. "But watch where you stand and squat. Some of the plants could cause an allergic reaction if they come into contact with skin."

Eva hurried in the direction he'd indicated, her cheeks burning at his matter-of-fact words. While on assignment, Casey said she often peed while standing up. Some sort of invention that allowed a woman to pee like a man. It was quicker, less embarrassing, and didn't involve body parts coming anywhere near the ground. An advantage, Casey had said.

Eva hadn't understood, but *holy Finnian bats*, she did now. The moment she got to the resort, she intended to ask her friend to acquire one for her. Eva hunted for a spot, checked for bugs, and hurriedly took care of business before rejoining Saber. He gave a courtly bow and stood aside to let her pass.

Stupid males. Eva muttered under her breath and stomped past, following the trail with ease. The walking was much easier than it had been the previous day.

The squawks of birds arguing up ahead slowed her steps until she saw they were of a regular size. They sat low in a tree, feeding, and on a fruit she recognized. An edible fruit. Eva started running, flapping her arms and shouting to scare them off.

The birds took off in a flash of scarlet and black, their calls of protest even louder than before. Chattering in agitated caws, they resettled on higher branches, their beady eyes measuring her danger factor. A couple hopped closer, cocking their scarlet heads. Eva jumped and seized the nearest piece of fruit. She sank her teeth into the bright green flesh and savored the tangy juices running over her tongue.

"Wait." Saber's hand closed over her shoulder. "How do you

know it's safe?"

"I use these on my restaurant menu. We import them from the Tiraq mainland."

"Are you sure?"

"Positive. Oh!" Eva yanked away from him and darted to the fallen fruit on the ground. "Yarrow worms! A delicacy." She plucked one from the partially eaten Yarrow fruit and gobbled it down, the firm, meaty texture tainted with the flavor of the fruit that was the worm's main diet. "Diners pay a fortune for a meal of Yarrow worms. They're seasonal, but this season pickings have been slim." She handed a plump, wriggling yellow worm to Saber. "Have one. They're very nutritious."

Saber took it, his doubtful expression echoing in his pretty eyes. He stared at the wriggling worm before biting down with his sharp teeth and swallowing. "Not bad."

"The fruit is good too."

"We should pick some and keep moving."

"What's the hurry? We'll stop for a meal."

Saber shrugged and plucked several ripe yarrow fruit off a tree. He discarded one that the birds had pecked and chose several others, which he stuffed in his trews pockets.

Eva slapped at a bug and bit into a yarrow. She tossed away the central stone and searched for another. A loud muffled snort came from behind her, and she turned to glare at Saber. "What? You think it's funny that my ass is hanging out every time I move?"

"That wasn't me." Saber scanned the bushes and lifted his nose to scent the air.

Eva shrugged and went back to picking yarrow—until something burst from the undergrowth beside her.

Eva screamed and scrambled back. She caught the gray of fur as she tripped and sprawled backward on her ass, smelled the fetid scent of the creature as it came to an abrupt halt. Beady black eyes stared at her. Then it charged.

"Watch out!" Saber shouted, seconds before he scooped her off the ground. He thrust her up into the branches of a tree, tossing her with easy strength. The yarrow she held in her hand went flying. Eva gripped the limb and concentrated on not falling.

A second creature charged from the bushes, heading straight for Saber.

"Saber!"

Horrified, she watched. The bulky creatures ran on four feet and, she realized, had rough-looking bristles instead of fur or hair. Wicked, curling tusks protruded from both sides of their jaws, and they squealed and grunted with each charge. Saber dodged one, stumbling when the second caught his leg with its tusk.

Eva's breath caught as Saber raised his fist and punched the creature on its flat nose. A shrill squeal rent the air. The creature shook its massive head and charged again. Saber was going to get gored with those yellowed tusks. Her hand clapped over her mouth. *No. No!*

But Saber jumped aside, one mighty tusk just catching the fabric of his trews and ripped them up to his knee.

Fear clawed through her when the creatures pawed the ground and ran at Saber from opposite directions. "Watch your back, Saber!"

He jumped for the outstretched limb of a tree and swung upward, placing all his weight on the branch seconds before the animals reached him. They struck each other, full force in the face.

Admiration filled her when Saber swung from branch to branch, avoiding the fighting creatures until he came to a rest on the same tree limb where she perched.

"You're bleeding," Eva said, knowing if it weren't for Saber, she would've ended up trampled or gored by the creatures.

"I'm fine," he said. "Once I shift to my feline form I'll heal."

"Oh. Is that what you were doing yesterday?"

"When you accused me of flashing?" Saber winked and her

breath caught in amazement.

Apart from Pryce, men had never paid attention to her, not until she'd become a wealthy widow. Then they'd even resorted to brute force in an attempt to become her husband. She forced the horrid memories away, consigning them to the past where they belonged.

"Um, yes."

"Shifters always heal better if they can change to their other form. It's something to do with the transformation."

"Can all your family shift?"

"Yes, apart from my mother. Is that a problem?"

"I don't have difficulties with other races," Eva said.

"Good to know."

"I can't afford to alienate my customers. We're near a spaceport, and our customer base comes from all over the galaxy."

Below them, the creatures squabbled over fallen yarrow fruit.

"How long do you think we'll be trapped up here?"

"As long as it takes," Saber said.

Frustration sliced and diced Eva. "We're never going to get to civilization at this rate." She'd worked so hard, and now it seemed revenge was slipping from her grasp. "I need to get back home as soon as possible."

Saber cocked his head. "Why?"

"None of your business." Eva shifted her weight, trying to find a comfortable spot, and the branch creaked. She clutched at her wooden perch, a gasp of panic escaping.

"Don't move," Saber said in a calm voice as if he were discussing the weather patterns for the upcoming day.

A distinct crack sounded, and Eva let out a squeak of terror, gripping the branch even harder. Beneath her the creatures gobbled up the windfall of fruit while she swayed on the wobbly tree limb. "The branch is going to break."

"No, it will be fine. I'll move to another tree." Like a youngster playing on a swing toy, he reached for the next branch and swung over.

The branch made another ominous cracking sound. Eva shifted to the left then overcorrected to the right. She felt herself falling and shrieked at the top of her lungs. Her hands clung to the branch, and her shirt rode up, the cool breeze whistling over her bare ass.

"It's all right, Eva. The pigs have wandered off. You can drop."

"Pigs? Is that what they were? How do you know they're not going to wander right back?"

Saber grasped her by the hips and helped her down without commenting on the shirt riding up. He did, however, smooth his warm palm across one buttock as he set her on her feet.

"Stop trying to sneak a touch," she snapped.

"If you continue with your caterwauling, you'll attract their attention."

Eva consciously lowered her voice, but it still emerged with a hint of strident attitude. "You touched my bottom."

"I could have left you dangling or let you fall to the ground. I can put you back up there if it will make you feel any better about the situation."

"You think you're funny. You're not." Eva cast a cautious look in both directions and started down the narrow track. This time she kept a wary eye on both the sky and ground, and she didn't bother to check to see if Saber had decided to follow in her chosen direction.

A tiny red creature darted across the path in front of her, and Eva almost jumped out of her filthy socks. She patted her chest and took a deep breath, hoping to regulate her heartbeat.

"I hate this planet," she muttered. "Give me a dirty market full of thieves and purse grabbers any day. At least I know what to expect."

The cat-man trotted past her in feline form, and she glanced at his rear leg. He appeared fine, so obviously shifting to heal the wound inflicted by the pig thing had worked. He looked a little silly with his tied trews looped around his neck, but that was probably a wise idea. He didn't exactly have pockets.

The track led into a clearing, and a narrow valley lay before them. Beyond the valley, several mountains sat in a compact group. Eva came to a halt and stared at the purple plumes of smoke coming from the tops of the cone-shaped peaks. "Why are they smoking?"

Of course the black cat didn't answer. He continued moving down the path while she stared and attempted to unravel this new mystery. The trees growing in the valley held a pink tinge on their trunks and branches, which was an attractive contrast to the green of the foliage.

Eva resumed her trek and noticed the valley was alive with the calls of birds. The undergrowth on either side of the path rustled suspiciously, and Eva increased her pace while trying not to think about the horrors of the beasties inhabiting the bushes. She checked the path ahead, fear crowding in on her when she realized she couldn't see Saber. The man might be annoying, he might even be in league with the Dearbhorgaills, for all she knew, but at least he seemed to want to keep her safe for now. He was her best chance of escaping this mess in one piece.

Eva quickened her pace until she was practically running. She burst around a bend in the path and came to a screeching halt to avoid a collision with Saber. The cat let out a rumbling purr, and Eva froze.

What now? Why has he stopped?

"What's wrong?" she whispered, because something *was* wrong. She could feel it in her bones. Her fingers curled into his fur, and she found herself inching closer until her hip was pressed against him.

He made another low sound deep in his throat and rubbed his head against her arm, while Eva swung her gaze across the path.

Next, she swept the skies. If the big bird grabbed them again it could drop them anywhere, even in the middle of the sea, which held the potential for greater terror.

"I can't see anything," she whispered.

Saber made another low sound and pulled away. He padded down the trail, and she realized he'd simply been waiting for her. Warmth bloomed in the region of her chest. She could count on one hand the number of times other people had worried about her well-being. Eva found herself smiling, a smile so wide it hurt her mouth. She increased her pace to catch him once more.

They stopped to pick and feast on several different types of fruits and berries she recognized. Once her thirst and hunger were appeased, her mind finally focused on her various aches and pains. She could also smell herself, and it wasn't pleasant.

Saber, now in his two-legged form, stopped again. He grinned. "I think I can hear water," he said. "This way."

Eva followed him down the trail, her gaze going to his tight butt, outlined nicely in his black trews. His upper half remained bare, and that drew her gaze too. She'd never known a male like him, not one who continually drew her attention. He fascinated her, brought her curiosity to the fore and made her want to ask dozens of questions—including if he had accepted money from the Dearbhorgaills to kidnap her.

Maybe she'd attempt a few casual queries later tonight. They had to fill the hours of darkness somehow.

Memories of what they'd done this morning heated her cheeks. She wouldn't mind repeating that again either, although she was sure it couldn't be as spectacular as she remembered.

"There's the water," Saber said.

Eva had been so deep in thought and busy staring at Saber, she hadn't noticed the change in scenery. "What is that smell?"

"I'm not sure," Saber said. "There's steam coming off the water, so it must be some sort of hot spring due to the volcanoes. It can't be that hot though because there are birds swimming in the water. On Earth, the hot springs smell of sulfur, but this is a different scent. It's almost floral." He frowned and lifted his head, his nostrils flaring. "It reminds me of the scent of lavender, a plant on Earth. My grandmother used to grow it in her garden. She made oil from the flowers and used the dried petals in soaps."

"Do you see any flowers?" Eva asked, fascinated by the tiny snippets he revealed. They were so far outside what she knew.

"No. We'll go closer. If the water isn't too hot, we might be able to swim."

"Wash?"

Saber gave her a quick smile, and her heart beat a little faster. Looking at him when he smiled—the flash of white teeth and the tiny fan of lines around the outside of his eyes—did something to her. His smile softened his harshly carved face and made her want to grin in return. A foreign feeling. She'd seldom felt the need to laugh or smile—only for a brief period when she'd had Pryce. And rarely since Pryce had died.

The valley went quiet, and Saber froze.

"What is it?"

A piercing shriek from above answered her question.

Saber scooped her off her feet and thrust her beneath the drooping foliage of a tree. The skinny green and pink leaves blocked her vision, but she could hear the screeches of the bird flying overhead.

Saber squeezed under the low branches and hauled her trembling body into his arms. "It didn't see us," he said against her ear.

"God, I hope not. It can land in the valley."

"It could, but I think it's hunting different prey today. Listen."

Eva swallowed and listened. In the distance she could hear panicked squawks, the thunder of running feet. She recognized the high-pitched shriek of the big-ass bird, heard the *whop-whop* of its wings.

"Whatever the bird is hunting is running this way," Saber said. "Curl up. Make sure your limbs are well off the path."

Eva didn't need to be told twice. She curled against Saber's warm, strong body and concentrated on breathing. *Hellfire and Finnian bats.* After this adventure, nothing in the city would ever scare her again. Even the Dearbhorgaills were manageable—their reactions predictable compared to the creatures inhabiting this island.

The panicked sounds came closer and closer. Squawks. Screams. Fast-running feet. Dust rose as terrified birds thundered past their hiding place. The birds were big, and all she could see were strong legs that ran past as they headed for the safety of the forest.

Eva pressed her face against Saber's chest and breathed in his masculine scent. His strong arms wrapped around her trembling body, and she was fiercely glad of his presence.

The *whop-whop* of wings sounded closer now, and the number of birds sprinting past their hiding place had thinned. The old and the young bringing up the rear, Eva thought. The infirm.

A bird limped past, trying to go fast but unable. A smaller bird raced at its heels, frantic squawks filling the air. The *whop-whop* sound was almost on top of them now, and Eva trembled violently.

"It's all right," Saber said. "The bird can't get us while we remain under here. He's after easier prey."

Eva opened her eyes again and watched as a bird was plucked off the ground right in front of their hiding place.

A small blue missile shot under the tree and hit Eva's side. She screamed, her cry of terror cutting off abruptly as she heard the *whop-whop* of wings.

"It's another bird," Saber said. "It's as scared as you are."

Eva swallowed, felt the bird quivering against her side. She shifted her position in a measured way so as not to cause fear and glanced down. The bird was bright blue with stout legs. Without haste, she reached out and stroked her hand over its blue feathers. The bird moaned, or at least the sound came close to one, and tried to squeeze closer.

"I think it's a baby," Saber said.

Eva croaked in dismay. "Is everything big on this planet?"

"So it would seem." Amusement colored Saber's voice and she became aware of something poking into her hip.

"Is that you?"

"Afraid so," he said without apology.

"That's disgusting."

"You didn't think so this morning."

Eva changed the subject. "Do you think the big-ass bird is gone? I can't hear anything now."

"Wait until we hear the other birds singing," Saber said. "That way we'll know it's safe."

"I'd love to have a wash."

"We will, as long as it's safe."

Eva relaxed and stroked her hand over the quivering bird that cuddled against her so trustingly.

"Have you seen one of these birds before?"

"No, there aren't any on the resort side of the island. Not big like this. We have the smaller variety."

"Maybe you should start running adventure tours," Eva said. "*I* can do without this type of adventure, but there are lots of males in Dalcon who'd thrive on this stuff."

"We don't own this land," Saber said. "Although there's no reason why we can't look into purchasing it at a later date."

"What is your favorite color?"

"Why?" Saber asked.

"I need to distract myself. I'm conjuring all sorts of horrid scenarios, and most of them contain big-ass birds eating me."

"If it weren't so cramped under here, I could distract you in other ways."

"I have a baby bird sitting right next to me."

Saber's low chuckle sent warmth burrowing through her veins. The heat converged in one achy spot between her legs.

"My favorite color is blue. Cornflower blue," he added.

"What color is that? I'm not familiar with that shade."

"It's the same shade as your eyes."

"Oh." The warmth spread upward and clawed dangerously close to her heart. Saber was a tricky man, and she'd do well to remember that.

"The birds have started singing again," Saber said.

Eva listened and realized he was right. "You think it's safe to crawl out of here?"

"I can't hear the wing-beat of the bird any longer. Stay here while I check."

Saber wriggled from beneath the tree, and Eva watched him walk along the trail until she could no longer see him. Her hand smoothed over the feathers of the bird cuddled against her, and she waited.

Saber scented the air and scanned his surroundings. He knew the danger was gone, since he saw the big pale-blue birds exit the trees and return to the grasslands of the valley. Overhead, birds of smaller species flitted through the air, and in the distance, he saw several bovine-type animals lazing in the sun of an open meadow.

He made his way down to the water and dipped in a finger. It was pleasantly warm, steam drifting up in lazy tendrils. After no adverse effects, he stripped off and waded into the water. It smelled of lavender and felt silky against his skin. Beneath the surface, tiny pink fish appeared. They approached him warily, but when he didn't move, they swam closer.

One darted to his arm and nibbled at a dry scab. Another headed for his feet. They weren't biting. They were feeding on his dead skin. Interesting.

Saber let them nibble until one or two swam too close to his groin.

"That's close enough," he muttered and waded from the water. He pulled on his trousers and boots and strode back to where he'd left Eva. "It's okay. You can come out."

"Where have you been?"

"I checked the water. It's safe to swim."

Eva slid from beneath the tree and groaned as she straightened. "*Ow.*" She shook her arms and legs and checked her elbow, frowned at a red scratch. "Swimming? Really?"

"You should be able to wash your clothes too."

"Let's go."

A distinctive honk came from the bright-blue bird. It waddled over to where Eva stood and waited.

"You've made a friend."

"As long as it doesn't want to eat me." Eva cast the bird a doubtful look, and Saber wanted to laugh. The bird had long, stout legs and a plump body. Its beak reminded him of a goose's, but the pale-violet color was distinctly alien. The blue feathers acted like a homing beacon, standing out against the mainly green grasses, and at the base they bore the same violet hue as the creature's beak.

"It reminds me of a goose on stilts. They're Earth grazing birds," he added.

"Oh." Eva's doubtful expression didn't shift. "I guess it will find its family soon. Where is this water? Lead the way."

The path leading to the swimming hole was wide enough for them to walk side by side. Saber placed his hand on the small of Eva's back and guided her in the right direction. Although she jolted when his fingers touched her skin, she didn't protest.

Maybe he was playing things too safe. Maybe he should give in to the impulses riding him to touch her—and touch her often.

"Why is the water steaming?"

"It's warm."

The bird honked and trotted after them. Eva glanced over her shoulder and frowned, but Saber urged her to continue walking.

At the water's edge, he bent to pull off his boots then waded into the water.

Eva hesitated.

"Take off your clothes if you want. I don't mind." Hell no. He didn't mind looking at her one bit. While some people might call her body boyish, she still had plump breasts. He suspected she didn't eat much and once he fed her properly, she'd become pleasingly curvy. Either way, he didn't care. She amused him, made him laugh.

The blue bird wandered off and started to graze, letting out intermittent honks. Eva had decided to strip, and Saber waded a little deeper into the water so his shoulders were submerged. The tiny pink fish were already nibbling his upper body, and he kept his gaze on Eva. Maybe he should warn her.

"*Flying Finnian bats,*" she said. "This feels so good."

It was good from his side too. Her breasts, with their pale-pink nipples, bobbed in the water. She scrubbed her hands over her body, under her arms, and groaned.

"Ooh, look," she said. "There are fish. I wonder if they're edible."

Saber bit back his amusement as he moved closer to her. She was about to discover *she* was dinner.

"They're a pretty color." She reached out a hand then let out a startled shriek. She lurched about in the water, her arms flapping and breasts bouncing. "I thought you said this was *safe?*"

She threw herself at him, arms clutching his shoulders, legs curled around his waist.

"Careful," he gasped while attempting to stem his urge to laugh long and loud. "You're cutting off my circulation."

"The fish are biting me!"

"They're nibbling at dead skin cells," he corrected. "Hold still and watch."

Eva stilled but remained wrapped around him. He watched her face, her blue eyes going round as the fish approached and started gently nibbling on her arm.

"It tickles."

"But they're not going to hurt you." Saber lifted an arm and stroked his fingers over her damp hair. "Want me to wash your hair for you?"

"You'd do that?"

"Lean your head back so I can wet your hair." He helped her float and supported her with one hand while he ran the fingers of the other through her locks. He massaged her head and saw her eyelids lower. After a few minutes, he'd washed it as best he could without soap. "All done. I'm going to take off my trousers and lay them on the bank to dry. I'll be back soon."

Her eyes flew open. A furrow etched between her brows.

"Don't worry, kitten. You'll be fine. I won't be far away."

Saber waded to the bank, and the blue bird came scurrying over, honking and rubbing against Saber's wet legs. "Hey, fella." He knelt and ran his hand over the bird's plumage. The honking turned to soft sighs, and when Saber stopped petting the bird, he pecked his leg, making a different sound yet again, almost demanding. "Funny blue bird."

Saber peeled off his trousers and draped them on a bush. The bird shuffled over to Saber's boots and sat between them. His head dropped to his chest, and his eyes closed. Saber shook his head and waded back into the water. He had the feeling that they might have found a third member to add to their party of two.

He headed straight for Eva. She was floating on the surface, her blonde hair fanned around her head. He noticed her legs were firmly together, and only a few tiny fish were feasting on her arms. He waded closer, slicing through the water with nary a splash until he reached her side.

Enticed by her breasts, he ducked his head and closed his mouth around one pert nipple.

"Oh!" She started floundering.

"Steady. I have you." *More than you realize.* Saber shoved the thought aside in favor of seduction. He took her mouth—hard and hungry. A play of teeth and lips until she responded, opening to him, letting him explore as she explored in return.

When he lifted his head, her lips were pink and swollen, her eyes large, dark pools of arousal and emotion.

Mine. Mine! he thought, his cat flexing powerfully beneath his skin. He hauled her into his arms, let her feel the steely length of his dick. His mouth closed around one nipple and he sucked strongly, drawing small noises of enjoyment from Eva. She wrapped wet limbs around him, clutching his head in a powerful grip.

Saber lifted his head and laughed. The joy of the unfamiliar sound wrapped around him, made him smile wider. He waded to the shore, the tiny fish swimming away, alarmed by the movement. Saber scanned the vicinity for signs of danger and saw nothing to alarm him.

He set Eva gently on a grassy bank and stood again, looming over her. "Spread your legs. I want to see you."

She stared at him for a long moment, hesitating.

"Do it," he ordered.

She frowned then parted her legs to reveal sexy pink flesh. A delicate tinge of pink flooded her cheeks, charming him.

"Don't be embarrassed. You're gorgeous." He squatted beside her and ran a light finger down her cleft until his fingertip came to a halt on her clit. It was swollen and stood out from its protective hood. "Beautiful."

"I...ah..."

"Shush, Eva. Your flesh is swollen and a deep pink color. You're so aroused."

"Um..."

"No talking, kitten. Just feel."

Saber lay between her legs and blew a stream of warm air over her flesh. Then he lifted her to his mouth and settled in to feast. Her tart flavor burst over him while her throaty moans urged him to greater liberties. He ran his tongue around her clit and pushed a finger into her moist channel. Beneath his skin, his feline twisted, urging him to act.

Saber froze as his canines grew longer—far more prominent than normal.

Fuck. That had never happened before.

"Is something wrong?"

He lowered his head again and gave her nub a firm lick in response. Eva's hands slid into his hair, holding him in place. The firm tugs grounded him, helped him exert control over his feline and push him back.

"More," she gasped. "That feels so good. Rough yet *so good*."

His feline stirred again, making his tongue raspy. Saber slid the tip around and over her clit. Eva gave throaty moans and yanked his hair to a point just shy of pain. He smiled as he pushed a second finger inside her and stroked while licking firmly. Her channel squeezed his fingers. He gave her another firm lick, and she cried out.

"Saber!" Her hips twitched and jerked beneath his touch.

Saber stroked her through her climax and removed his fingers once her spasms ceased.

He rose up her body and kissed her, slow and deep. God, he couldn't get enough of her. Her scent, her taste, the feel of her hands running over his body. He rolled until she sprawled on top of him.

"Take me inside you," he ordered, his hands grasping her hips in silent demand. When she hesitated, he lifted her. He guided his cock to her entrance and lifted his hips. "Take me inside you!"

She smiled—a siren's smile as she pushed down and took his cock. Saber gripped her hips and groaned at the warm heat encircling him. "Damn, that feels so good. You're so tight and hot." *Mine. All mine.* "Move. Don't tease me. Ride me, kitten."

Saber helped her set a blistering pace, savored the wet heat around his sensitive tip. He spanned her hips with his hands, allowing the feel of her to ground him even as he pounded upward over and over and took his pleasure. He slipped one finger between her legs and rubbed her clit.

She gasped, and when her sheath tightened around him, he exploded into his climax. His gaze remained fastened on her as he came, and he watched her fly apart, pleasure suffusing her cheeks and tinting even her breasts with delicate color.

She collapsed against his chest, and his arms wrapped around her, holding her in place. His possessive manner wasn't lost on him, but she didn't seem to notice. Her eyes fluttered closed, and her breathing became slow and regular.

"Kitten, wash then I'll find a safe place for us to sleep while I scout for food."

She made a noncommittal murmur, and Saber smiled. He parted their bodies and carried her back into the water. He bathed her, washing between her legs while part of him wished neither of them had taken health inoculations to prevent conception. The idea of her swelling with his child was an attractive one, and something he hoped would happen in the future.

Hell, this time with Eva might not have been planned, but it felt right on so many levels. Already the idea of parting from her agitated his feline, and didn't do much for his mood either.

Eva was his. They belonged together. And soon, she'd come to understand the truth of it, just as he did.

CHAPTER SIX

E xperience had Eva scanning her surroundings to check for
signs of danger before she found a comfortable spot to dry
off. She'd washed her shirt and socks, and now they were drying in
the bright solar shine.

The blue bird followed, settling beside her with a sound that
hovered between a contented sigh and a honk.

Eva checked the area again before letting her mind wander.
Flying Finnian bats, she hated being out of contact with her
assistant. Missed the bustle of her restaurants. Though one thing
she didn't yearn for was the constant specter of her in-laws,
while she waited for them to make yet another grabby move
for her restaurants. If only she hadn't been so inexperienced at
first. Pryce's sudden death had left her floundering. She'd made
mistakes, and she was still paying for them.

As soon as they reached the resort, she'd take a flight to Dalcon, check out the situation, see where her plans were at, and what she needed to do next.

The blue bird got tired of napping and wandered off to graze on a patch of grass. Eva watched it before her mind wandered again to her plan. She'd saved enough to pay the next installment of the loans taken out to purchase her third restaurant, the one that Pryce had negotiated for before his death.

Wanting to honor her husband, she'd attempted to borrow money herself to make the third restaurant a reality. Pryce's parents had blocked her attempts to get a loan from a reputable source, and in her desperation, she'd borrowed from a nontraditional one.

Too late, she discovered she'd borrowed money from her in-laws.

The moment she defaulted on a payment, they'd be entitled to step in and take everything she and Pryce had worked so hard for.

Her hands fisted as her mind dwelled on the worst-case scenario. Wasn't going to happen. Not if she had her way. She'd die first. She owed it to Pryce.

A largish bird soared through the valley. Eva tensed, but when Bluebird continued to graze, she relaxed. He, or she, seemed to know when danger was nearby, so perhaps Eva could sleep a little.

She woke abruptly, every part of her body tense. Her heart smacked against the wall of her chest, her muscles locked in terror when the weird crunching sound came again, along with a sharp honk.

Eva turned her head, took in the situation swiftly—and fury replaced her fear. "A pox on it! A pox on bloody Saber Mitchell, may his dangle rot and fall off!" She sprang to her feet and advanced on Bluebird, flapping her hands. "Shoo! Shoo!"

Bluebird squawked and backed away, the remains of a com-circle in his beak. She made a grab for it, but he crunched down, and it broke into two parts. One dropped to the ground. She swooped on it and glared at the electronic innards.

He'd had a com-circle the entire time. And now it was broken.

That was it.

She'd known trusting him was foolish. Males... She should have learned her lesson by now. If she wanted a job done, it was best for her to do it herself.

Eva stomped to her shirt and pulled it on. She sat, scowling, her hands trembling as she pulled on the socks. Eva jumped to her feet, frowned left, and glared right. She glowered at the sky, doing a slow three-sixty to check for big-ass birds.

All clear.

Eva chose a direction and set off to rescue herself. To hell with Saber. She didn't intend to sit around and wait to discover his sneaky plan.

Saber arrived back at the waterhole much later than he'd expected. He'd found several fruit trees and cursed himself for not bringing his trousers. Difficult to carry stuff in feline form without a receptacle of some sort.

The solar light had almost faded when he prowled up to the waterhole, a hastily woven bag tied around his neck.

Eva wasn't there.

He dumped his bag of fruit and shifted. "Eva? Eva?"

When she didn't come out of hiding, concern gave way to fear. When he'd left her, she'd been lying in the dappled sunshine. He thought she'd be safe enough since the few trees at the edge of the water could hide her from predators circling overhead.

He went to grab his trousers, and something sharp dug into the sole of his foot. He bent to pull it out. "Fuck!"

Eva had discovered he was in possession of a communicator. That put her absence in a different light.

Damn, why did women have to make a situation so difficult?

Things had been going well between them. Maybe she wouldn't hold a grudge.

He considered grudges and women for a few seconds, then his mouth twisted into a snarl. *Yeah, right.*

He tied his trousers and his boots around his neck with practiced skill. Seconds later, he was circling the area in feline form, searching for her scent. He found it soon enough and realized the blue bird had followed her.

Nose to the ground, he increased his speed to a lope and followed Eva's trail.

Once the solar light disappeared, the temperature dropped. At least it wasn't raining. Eva trudged through the darkness, her nerves jumping at each new sound. Bluebird practically hugged her leg, never more than a beak-length away, which told her he was scared too. She needed to find a safe place to spend the night. Not a cave. But maybe at the base of a tree. Some of the bigger trees were hollowed out. She started scanning each one she passed, saw a possible, and approached with quiet, cautious steps.

Bluebird honked, and she paused. "One honk for yes and two honks for no," she said.

Bluebird obediently honked. Three times.

"What does that mean?"

The bird remained silent.

"An unreliable warning system," she mumbled. Already, she'd learned to expect the unexpected in the cursed jungle. "Here goes," she said, approaching the hollow sanctuary with trepidation. "Why does it have to be so dark?" She peered inside.

Two golden eyes stared back.

Eva froze. "Uh, sorry to disturb you." Holding her breath, she backed away. "Please don't attack. Please don't. Please don't."

Bluebird let out three low honks.

"Okay, I get it. Three honks means already occupied."

Wearily, she trudged along the narrow trail and searched for another haven. Despite the lower temps, sweat ran down her forehead, beaded between her breasts. Her heavy feet found every sharp rock on the path. What felt like hours later, she discovered a tree with exposed roots. It offered both concealment and shelter from the worst of the wind that tugged her hair, swirled leaves, and ruffled treetops to create creepy noises.

Bluebird ran straight into the shelter, so she figured it was safe enough. She scooped up some leaf litter to make a sort of a bed and settled in. Bluebird honked, a sound of contentment, she decided, and cuddled against her chest.

It was so cold, but at least the wind wasn't cutting through her shirt and nipping at her bare flesh any longer. Eva listened to the rustle of the leaves, the moan of the wind as it wended its way through the trees. Occasionally, a growl or a squawk jerked her to full terror instead of her current low-level fear.

When she settled everything in Dalcon, she was going to take a long break. She'd buy herself the biggest, most lethal weapon money could buy, and she'd return to Middlemarch Resort and shoot Saber's sexy ass full of holes. And she'd enjoy doing it because this was all his fault. Every last bit of her precarious position.

She'd walked farther than he'd expected. Saber lost her trail once but managed to pick it up again. At least she was still in one piece and moving, but he worried about her alone in the dark. There were some big predators out here, and they were lucky they hadn't crossed paths with many of them. *Yet.* The last thing he needed was for Eva to face danger on her own.

Her trail stopped, then started again, and Saber's opinion of her grew. She was looking for a place to hole up and wait out the night.

Clever lady.

He'd already known she was smart and determined, and now he could add resourceful and intelligent.

Saber lost the scent for a while and circled back looking for it again. Then he saw Eva, and relief swept through him, making his four legs tremble.

He did a quick shift, wrapped his trousers in a tight ball and placed his boots within easy reach. She must have been exhausted because she didn't wake when he squeezed in beside her and drew her into his arms.

The bird gave a sleepy honk and settled back to doze.

Saber listened to the jungle sounds and relaxed. Eva had chosen well. They were safe enough here for the rest of the night.

Eva woke feeling warm. Bluebird still cuddled into her chest, making breathy little sounds. A birdy type of snore.

But the warmth at her back, the hand at her hip...

She stiffened and struck, raking the hand with her clawed fingers.

"*Ow!* What did you do that for?"

Eva twisted, disturbing Bluebird and wriggling free of Saber's arms. She sprang to her feet, putting distance between them. "You're lucky I'm not a titled lady. Their fingernails are filed to stabby points. You had a com-circle! You had one all the time. You could have called for help. How much are the Dearbhorgaills paying you? *How much*?"

"No one is paying me anything," Saber said.

He was smart to look wary. Her hands bunched into fists as she imagined throttling him. "You bastard," she spat. "You knew I wanted to go home. I've made that very clear. How far are we from the resort? Tell me."

"We're on the other side of the island," Saber said.

"Is anyone coming to get us?"

Saber hesitated.

"*Flying Finnian bats!*" she snarled.

"What's a Finnian bat?"

"They're dirty, rotten, cheating scumbags," she snapped. "Just like you."

"Ouch," he said.

"This isn't a laughing matter."

"I don't believe I was laughing."

"Ooh! I can't look at you." She whirled away before turning back with a fierce scowl. "At least tell me if I'm going the right way. Give me that much, at least."

"If you promise not to stab me in the back, I'll lead."

Eva glared and folded her arms over her chest. "Put your trews on. I'm tired of looking at your dangly thing."

He smirked. "Not so much of the dangly."

"I'm going to find a bush. When I come back, you will point me in the direction of the resort. That is all I require from you."

Eva stomped to a bush and took care of business. This was the third day. She had a solar week before things would become desperate. Her assistant would contact Casey if he couldn't communicate with her. She could count on her best friend to look after her interests. While Casey might not know the details, she knew it was important for Eva to get back to Dalcon before the start of the next solar month.

"Want some fruit?"

Eva snatched the glossy pink fruit from him and bit down without a word of thanks. Bluebird honked, and Saber shrugged.

84

He gave her an insolent wink and stalked off along an overgrown path.

Eva forced her body to move and trudged after him. She'd thought she was reasonably fit from cooking and working long hours in the restaurants. Not so. Every part of her body ached, and she couldn't wait to have a proper meal. This fruit stuff wasn't very filling.

"How do you know where you're going?"

"I don't. We're heading to the east, which is toward the resort."

"Tell me the truth. How many solar days will it take us to reach the resort?"

Saber slowed and glanced at her over his shoulder. "Four. Maybe five."

He wasn't lying. She read the truth in his face. Her shoulders drooped momentarily before she gave herself a stern lecture. She'd spent her childhood in the market. She'd clawed her way into a successful business. She could handle a few more solar days with Saber Mitchell.

If she didn't give in to impulse and murder him first.

If she lost the restaurants because of him...

Eva forced her mind away from her problems, the bloody ticking timepiece in her brain that was counting down the nanoseconds to disaster.

She ground her teeth and concentrated on Bluebird walking in front of her. The bird waggled its tail feathers with each step—a sort of cute twitch. Her gaze wandered and settled on Saber's butt.

She jolted, scowled, looked away. She didn't need to see the firm flex of his muscles.

Bluebird released a shrill squawk, and Saber cursed.

"We need to hide. It's those damn birds again." Saber grasped her upper arm and propelled her toward the shelter of a large tree. He scooped her into his arms when she tripped and sprinted the rest of the way.

"Thanks." The word was clipped and held not a shred of real sentiment.

"You're welcome."

He was laughing at her. "It's your fault I'm in this mess," she snapped. "If it weren't for you, I wouldn't be in the middle of nowhere, half naked and starving, with a big-ass bird wanting to snack on me."

The humor disappeared from his face as they reached the tree. "I'm sorry."

Above them, the large bird screeched. Bluebird honked, a low call of distress, and Eva stooped to pet him. "It's okay, fella. We're not going to let anything happen to you."

"He'd taste good roasted over a fire."

"That's not funny."

"We need to find food. You can't afford to lose any more weight."

"My weight needn't concern you," she said in a frosty voice. "I think the bird has gone now. Can we get moving?"

Saber checked the skies. "Of course. There are some fruit trees at the end of the valley."

"Which way do we go once we leave the valley?"

"We continue east."

No hesitation. Yes, she thought he was telling the truth. But she didn't trust Saber and began forming her own plan. He didn't have her best interests in mind, and he *still* hadn't told her why he'd kidnapped her. While she suspected the Dearbhorgaills were involved, he hadn't confessed. Not yet.

No, she couldn't trust him. And she didn't have to stick with him either. At the first opportunity, she'd strike out on her own once more.

"How did you find me?" she asked, feigning nonchalance.

He slid another glance over his shoulder and grinned before turning his attention back to the path. "I followed your trail. Once

I caught your scent, it was easy to find you."

"I see." She wasn't stupid. She wouldn't make the same mistake again.

CHAPTER SEVEN

S omething was up with Eva. He couldn't put his finger on the what, but she was too quiet and had been too biddable for the last two days.

They'd covered a lot of ground, more than he'd expected they would. After another two days of trekking, they'd reach the resort or at least one of the small towns on the coast, where he was positive they'd find transport.

Not much longer to seduce her to his way of thinking.

At least she was sleeping close to him during the nights, even though she said it was to keep warm. He breathed in her scent, fresh and green after they'd bathed at another pool. She murmured in her sleep, and he drew her closer

Bluebird stirred and shambled out of their resting place—an old lava cave. Other birds were calling in a dawn chorus.

Saber ran a hand over Eva's hip and nuzzled her collarbone. He kissed the soft skin and aimed a second kiss at her lips. She gave a sleepy groan and turned into his arms.

For an instant, he froze, then he went with the moment, arranging her firmly against him and settling in to kiss the hell out of her. Fuck. She was so sweet. Even when she was giving him the silent treatment, she amused him, made him think about their future.

Kids.

Pets.

His own family.

Hell, they had the pet thing sorted already, although he'd been thinking more along the lines of a cat or a dog or the local equivalent. His brothers were gonna laugh their asses off when they saw Bluebird.

She gave another sleepy groan and wrapped her arms around his neck. Her breasts flattened against his chest, and he gave in to temptation and slid his hand under the ragged shirt to explore the silky skin beneath. He pinched a nipple and felt it harden beneath his fingertips.

Unable to resist, he slipped a hand lower to smooth over her butt, then rolled her beneath him, parting her legs with his thigh. She froze for a second, and he thought she'd nix his plan for some morning loving, but she surprised him by relaxing again and giving him free access to her body.

Saber fingered her, teasing her until she moaned, and her folds became slippery with her arousal. He sucked her neck, taking pleasure in the act, knowing he'd see his mark of ownership later in the day.

With increasingly urgent hunger and a pleasurable ache in his balls, he rose over her and pushed deep inside her. Her snug channel flexed around him while she encouraged his thrusts by placing her hands on his ass. Desire kicked in his belly, urged him to move faster, shove deeper and harder. He resisted, wanting to give Eva pleasure first, make this good for her. His hand tangled in the hair at her nape, and he claimed her mouth, giving her steady thrusts at what he hoped was the perfect angle.

The hands at his butt tightened, fingernails dug into his flesh. She cried out against his mouth, gasped hard, and came in a violent spasm of pleasure.

Thank you, God. Saber increased his pace, plunging into her with hard thrusts. Words spilled from his lips. "Fucking you is heaven, Eva. I love the feel of your sheath around my dick. The husky sounds you make and the fuckin' sweet way you give me pleasure." Dirty words. Explicit words.

Nothing less than the truth.

She made him feel whole, completed him, but those words he'd utter another time.

Later. Later, he'd let his real personality shine through once she stopped acting like a flighty filly ready to flee at a moment's notice. Or maybe that was where he was going wrong. He was being so careful with her. Maybe he should loosen his restraint and act the alpha male.

"Feel so good enveloping my cock. So wet. Tight. Just fuckin' perfect." His lustful thoughts spilled out. The hands bruising his backside dug into the muscle, and the liquid heat surrounding his dick seemed to grow hotter, her arms clutching him in a tight embrace. "Wanna fuck that sassy mouth of yours. Your ass."

Mine, he thought. *My woman.* Not that he'd say it aloud. Not yet. He still had some self-preservation. Instead he concentrated on chasing his orgasm.

"One day, I want to fuck you in a big, soft sleep-bed. Maybe after I've taken you on the kitchen counter." His cock seemed to lengthen as he growled the words into her ear, his balls pulling painfully tight.

"That is not very sanitary," she said in a prissy voice. "Kitchens are for food and cooking."

"You got cleaning products in that kitchen of yours?" Saber pulled back, pushed home, and groaned, coming so hard he saw stars. Pink ones, which made no sense at all because that was a girlie color.

"Of course," she gasped.

Saber withdrew a fraction and growled again at the sensations that jerked his cock. Long moments later, when the contractions trailed off, he pulled out of her and arranged her on his chest like a living blanket. "You got cleaning products, then we're having sex on the counter. I'm gonna drape you over and take you from behind."

His feline rolled under his skin, and Saber gave an involuntary thrust against her leg. "You got another one in you?"

"Again? I'll start waddling like Bluebird."

"You got another one?"

He slipped a finger between her legs, gave a slow, firm rub, watching her eyes all the while. Long dark lashes lowered, but not before he saw the deep blue of her eyes. She wanted him.

"Don't you think we should start walking instead of lazing about in a cave?"

Saber didn't answer, merely drew her head down and laid one on her. Lips, teeth, tongue. He gave it everything and almost cheered when she softened and started responding.

"Ride me. Take what you need."

"But you've just—"

He lifted her a fraction and set her down over his groin, right where she could feel his interest. Her lashes lifted, giving him a great view of her sexy blue eyes.

"There's something wrong with you."

"Ain't nothing wrong with me. All my parts are working fine. Wanna have you again before we start our day."

He lifted her, holding her up while he waited for her to obey his silent demand. She just stared, her mind working in ways mysterious to him since she kept her features expressionless. He figured it was a strategy she'd learned in the market. Don't let anyone know your thoughts because knowledge gives them the advantage.

"I can tell you exactly what to do," he said.

She tilted her head. "You haven't before."

"A mistake on my part." Saber waited until their gazes connected. "Take my cock—now."

She bit her lip, a hint of uncertainty creeping into her face.

"Then ride me hard. I want you to feel me when you walk, and I want to smell me on you. I like that."

The uncertainty shifted into incredulousness. "It sounds as if you want to own me."

Saber felt a slow grin take residence on his face and guessed his eyes sparkled with the same smugness beating in his heart. "I do," he said quietly. "But the chase is fun too."

Her mouth turned mulish, and he figured he'd pushed a bit far. Too bad. This was him.

He rolled her under him, made sure she lay on the bed of soft grasses he'd collected the previous night, and pushed his knees between her legs. He thrust inside her, watching her face. He started slow, using every bit of his expertise to tease another orgasm out of her. She was slippery and wet, liquid heat around his dick.

When she started responding, digging her fingers into his shoulders and making sexy little moans at the back of her throat, he increased his pace and took his pleasure. They came together, not as hard as the first time, but still ultimately satisfying.

Saber smoothed her blonde hair off her forehead and placed a gentle kiss on the skin he revealed. "I could go again if you're interested."

"I'm sore," she whispered, her words hot against his throat. "And I believe I smell like you, both inside and out. Goal achieved."

"Good," he said, choking back a snigger. "My work here is

done."

Saber, the cat-man, was kinda hot. She'd have some great memories once she arrived back on Dalcon.

Casey would be pleased she'd finally had sex. During one inebriated night years ago, Casey had told her it wasn't good to let your lady parts dry out. Gave guys the wrong idea. Made them think you didn't enjoy sex and didn't care if you ever had sex again.

Recalling the words now, Eva worried slightly about Casey. When she saw her again—*if* she saw her friend before she reported for duty—Casey would demand answers to her pointed questions. She had been there for her when Pryce died and had helped her with decisions, even though they'd been on different planets. It was time for Eva to repay the debt of friendship.

She pushed against Saber's shoulders and wriggled out from under him. After dressing, she scuttled outside to find a bush. This outdoor plumbing was the pits. If she had money, she'd buy one of those climatic suits. Regulated body temperature and took care of everything else too. Casey wore them on some of her missions.

Business done, she needed to ponder her escape. Saber was dragging his heels, slowing her down. But she'd escape the smug cat-man if it was the last thing she did. She'd pop his arrogance balloon and shove his nose in her success, should they ever meet again.

Saber Mitchell wasn't going to best her.

The Dearbhorgaills weren't going to beat her.

She would triumph.

They rounded the base of one of the volcanoes during their morning walk. The air was full of a strange scent, something Saber said was sulfur. Ugh, the stench reminded her of a rotten *dravy* egg. She picked her way around rocks and boulders, wincing when a sharp piece of rock dug into her big toe. The socks were wearing thin and wouldn't last much longer. Wearing the same shirt for solar days was as annoying as her lack of undergarments, although Saber had remarked on the convenience.

In the distance, in the valley they'd traveled through previously, a herd of large grazing animals was visible, plus the usual flocks of birds, much bigger and leggier versions of Bluebird, who also fed on the grasses and plants.

They climbed a rise, the day's heat sticking her shirt to her sweaty skin. Saber came to an abrupt stop and swore.

"What is it?"

He pointed at the red river that flowed from the top of one of the cones. It glowed and sparkled in the solar light as it oozed down the slope.

"And I repeat," she said. "What is it?"

"A lava flow. We won't be able to cross it. We'll have to walk around it. That way looks best."

She followed his gesture with his gaze and groaned. "We have to go around the base of *that* smoking hill too?"

"I think so."

"What happens if there's another one on the other side?"

"There's not much cover that way," Saber said. "Those birds are always flying over. We need hiding places."

"My socks aren't much protection against these rocks. The rocks in that direction are worse." Hopelessness threatened to buckle her knees, and she staggered to a shady spot and sank to the ground.

Bluebird followed and settled in beside her with a contented honk.

"I'm so tired," she whispered. "I don't think I've ever been this tired."

Saber frowned at her and glanced in the direction he'd proposed they travel. "Why don't I shift and check out the route? If it's viable, I'll come back to get you. You can rest out of the sun."

"Thank you," she said and closed her eyes. "Do you think it will take you long? Will I have time for a sleep?"

"You can sleep, kitten."

Eva sighed, her weariness evident. "Thanks."

"You can use my trousers as a pillow," he said. "Don't let Bluebird play with my boots."

"I'll put them under your trews. Try not to be too long." A nice touch, Eva thought as she opened her eyes and reached for his trews and boots.

Saber's smile was tender when he stooped to steal a kiss, and a flash of temper boiled inside her. She had difficulty restraining a snappish retort. "Take care."

"You too, kitten. Keep under the cover of the rocks in case the birds fly over while you're asleep."

"It might be cooler under those two trees down there. They should be okay for a screen."

He glanced at them and gave a swift nod. "See you soon."

She watched him transform to cat, the sucky and crunchy sounds a little freaky, although she had to admit his cat shape was very sexy.

He gave a low grunt and loped off. Eva waited until he disappeared, then waited for a little more time to pass before climbing to her feet. She was tired. True. But not too tired to seize the opportunity he'd given her to escape. "Happy birthday to me," she muttered and slapped the dust off her butt.

She checked her surroundings for danger, noted Bluebird appeared relaxed and untroubled and set off in the other direction. Hopefully, Saber was wrong, and the fiery river ended or thinned enough for her to cross safely.

Eva kept to the tree line as much as possible and found a wide path, which made traveling swift and easy. She passed other varieties of animals but took her cues from Bluebird. If he scuttled for cover, she followed suit.

She stopped to collect some fruit and ate it as she continued, knowing it was best for her to put as much distance as possible between them because Saber would attempt to track her. She came to water—a narrow stream—and after checking it for obvious predators, she waded into the middle and used its meandering path as a trail, hoping that might confuse the arrogant cat-man.

Bluebird honked from the bank then wandered off to graze. Eva wasn't worried since he did this often and always seemed to find them at day's end.

She continued walking until the roar in the distance told her the stream took a tumble over rocks. She clambered out and surveyed the copse of pink and blue trees and the vivid lilac and green bushes. The bushes bore long, deep-purple pods. A type of nut sold in the market and one of her favorite treats.

"Yum, your birthday lunch is served." She would pick a few handfuls and eat them on the move.

She limped over to the nearest bush and started picking the nuts, working her way around...

And coming face-to-face with a trio of bipeds.

They didn't look a bit like Eva. Their brows and facial features were much more prominent, and most of their visible skin was a bright pink-red. Light-brown hair covered their arms, legs, and torsos—too light to be called fur but heavier than anything she'd witnessed before. The closest one had a nose piercing, and they were obviously female since they had breasts like hers. Apart from the fuzzy hair on their bodies, they wore no other clothing.

"Hello," she said, focusing on their faces while trying not to stare. "I'm pleased to see you. Can I purchase transport to get to the resort on the other side of the island?"

The females stared at her, their mouths opening to reveal yellowed incisors and fanglike canines. Eva looked more closely at the one with the pierced nose and swallowed hard. Was that a bone?

She took a step back and bumped into something.

Damn, Saber was fast, a better tracker than she'd given him credit for. And he had bad timing.

She stepped away and turned, ready to glare, and instead found two more bipeds. These had light-blue faces and...oh!

She let out an *eep* of shock and hurriedly backed away. The ones with blue faces had matching color on their groins. They were male. *Definitely* males because they hadn't bothered to hide their masculine equipment.

"Um, hi." She raised a hand, recalling Casey saying it was a universal greeting.

One of the males grunted, the guttural sound not reassuring. Neither was the way he grasped her upper arm, his sharp nail-like claws digging into her flesh.

She hoped that was some weird greeting. Eva took a deep breath and wished she hadn't. He needed to bathe. Still, she couldn't act with rudeness. She reached out her hand, noticed it was trembling but forged ahead. Her fingers banded his biceps, and she squeezed.

The females gasped in unison and took a collective step back.

Holy Finnian bats. Eva's hand fell to her side. "Um, I guess I'll be going. So sorry to bother you." She wouldn't ask about transport again. She wouldn't ask about the lava flow and how to get around it. She wouldn't dally to chat. Better not to ask questions, full stop.

Eva wrenched her arm free and darted around the group. No birthday lunch for her. She was leaving right now.

The males grabbed her before she passed the nut bushes. They hauled her to a stop despite her struggling. *Frying fungus,* the males stunk worse than a skunk-hen, and those were eye-wateringly bad on the stinkometer.

One of them jabbered something, the guttural clicks too much for her universal translator implant. All she got was gibberish. While she was puzzling over the communication—because she was *sure* this was a cultural misunderstanding, and she could fix it—the females approached.

The female with the bone through her nose said something and poked Eva in the stomach. They cackled together in discordant harmony. One of the males, who also possessed a decorative bone in his nose, squeezed her butt.

Eva didn't care what sort of cultural misunderstanding this was, *no one* groped her without permission. She swiftly lifted her right knee and kicked backward.

Her foot struck the male's groin front and center.

He bellowed and collapsed in a heap, his clawed hands holding his dangly as if it were broken.

She would've snorted, but Eva took the opportunity to run. Behind her, she heard a shout, and then thundering footsteps pounded the ground. Eva pushed harder, ignoring the branches and jagged stones. Her lungs burned, and her breaths came in harsh pants. She sprinted around the corner and came to an abrupt halt.

The lava stream ran across the track. Hot and deadly, it had annihilated everything in its path, toppling trees and burning the undergrowth. The lava carried a load of rocks and moved with pops and cracks and crunches like a grumpy conveyor belt. The nasty scent of sulfur and scorched plant materials hung in the air.

Eva turned to flee in the opposite direction. A line of blue-faced males stood between her and freedom.

The male with the bone in his nose barked something, and four males stepped forward. Eva released a nervous laugh, but it didn't hold much in the way of amusement. Four males to retrieve little old her. She remained rooted to the spot, unwilling to make things easy for them.

They approached warily. She glared and struck out, but ultimately to no avail. Two of them each grasped an arm and propelled her toward an unknown destination. The other two walked at a prudent distance behind, close enough to offer aid but far enough away to avoid smashed danglies.

One of the big birds wheeled through the air, and their leader shouted another order. The males hustled her into the trees and followed a less obvious trail through the undergrowth.

Interesting.

These people were wary of the birds too.

After a short distance, Eva spied a group of thatched huts. Smaller huts circled a much larger one. The males dragged her to one of the minor huts and thrust her inside. They shut the door after her, and she heard a series of orders, more rapid-fire clicks that drew a blank from her translator.

She circled the interior of the hut and noted the streams of light piercing the walls. Not thick. She'd bet she could muscle her way through or dig underneath. After examining her options, she decided on the latter and got to work, digging with her hands. It was surprisingly easy, and soon, she'd made a hole big enough to squeeze through. She sucked in a breath and squished beneath the gap.

A guttural sound lifted her head, and she rose to her feet. Bone Nose. He of the smashed danglies. Eva sighed.

This didn't seem to be her day.

Bone Nose grabbed her arm and dragged her around to the front of the hut, jabbering in clicks and squawks. Several females scurried off and returned with strands of pliable vines.

Uh-oh. This can't be good.

Bone Nose dragged her around the largest hut, and she saw two poles driven into the ground. A four-legged creature of a type she'd never seen before was tied to one pole. They tied Eva to the other, slapping her when she dared to struggle. Eva ignored the blows to her arms and legs, the high-pitched jabbers and continued to struggle until they finished their job.

As it turned out, the vines were soft yet very, very strong. *Flying Finnian bats.* She'd need a bloody miracle to get away from these furry maniacs.

Eva surveyed the area, mind busily working on an escape plan should a miracle present itself. Even though it meant backtracking and possibly running into Saber, he appeared the lesser of two evils.

Movement in the doorway of the large hut drew her attention. What the devil were they doing? Eva stared at the females as they dragged out a huge pot and left it beside a blackened fire pit.

The men went into the jungle and came back dragging bright-green tree branches. Others held armfuls of black logs. Eva watched them toil, hollow apprehension dancing in her stomach, pressing against her chest as they lit a fire. The entire time, she tugged at her bonds until her wrists ached and her muscles throbbed.

Once the flames grew bigger and caught the wood, the males set the pot over the fire. Some of the females approached carrying pails of water, and Eva frowned when they poured them into the pot.

It was an awfully *big* pot.

Her gaze shifted to the other pole and the wretched-looking creature that stood with its heavy head down, furry gray sides rising and falling in rapid pants.

Another female added a platter of root tubers while a second tipped in a pail of leafy herbs.

The chef in Eva toted up the ingredients and came up with various dishes. Stock pot, tubers, herbs—a stew of some sort.

The females jabbered amongst themselves and called over one of the males. They conducted a heated discussion. Eva didn't like the tone of their interaction or the way they kept looking in her direction.

Four of the males broke away from the group and stalked straight to her, determined expressions on their faces. Eva stiffened.

"Let me go. I haven't done anything. You have to let me go!"

Hope surged when they released her bindings and dragged her away from the pole.

"Thank you," she said and turned to walk away. If she hurried, she could get a good start before darkness fell.

Hard clawed fingers grasped her forearm and jerked her to a halt.

"*Frozen fungus*, what are you doing?"

Bone Nose jabbered something, and the males bound her and lifted her into the cooking pot.

Frozen fungus and flapjacks.

She was *dinner*! The meat to go with the veg.

She'd stepped from the fire and landed in the cooking pot.

The water wasn't hot yet—thank the goddess. *You're tough*, her inner cook suggested. *They're intending to cook you long and slow.*

Eva roared and started twisting from side to side. The pot didn't budge. She began shouting. "Help! Help! Help!"

One of the females cackled.

"Help!" Eva shrieked louder. The water was starting to get hot around her feet, and tendrils of steam were beginning to drift lazily off the surface of the cooking pot.

The woman cackled again, and all the tribe, including Bone Nose, cracked wide grins.

"Help!" Eva screamed.

Their grins spread and grew, turning into chuckles and ribald amusement at her expense. They slapped each other on the back and could hardly stand, so great was their hilarity. They thought her screams for help were hysterical.

Sweat dribbled down her forehead and into her eyes.

Oh, goddess. She was going to die in a cooking pot.

Saber heard Eva's screams and moved faster until he smelled something ripe. Rotten. He screeched to a halt and proceeded cautiously, his nose low to the ground as he worked out the scents. The pungent trail headed in the direction of Eva's shouts, and he increased his pace again.

At the edge of the clearing, he slowed and stalked closer, belly to the ground. He halted, partly concealed under a bush, and took in the scene in one quick glance.

Cannibals.

He'd have to take them by surprise, distract them. Damn, that cooking pot looked heavy. There was no way he could knock it over. He'd have to shift and lift her out.

No other option.

Saber bounded out of hiding and headed straight for Eva. He roared, his fury exploding into the clearing and causing chaos. In his peripheral vision, he saw the shock on their blue and red faces, their fear, and then the anger when they saw he intended to snatch their dinner.

Several of the taller ones leaped to action, murder in their eyes.

Time for stage two of his plan.

Saber called up his human form and willed it to be the quickest change ever.

His wish was granted, and an instant later, Saber stood in front of the pot, the sight of him stunning the males to a halt. He seized Eva and plucked her from the pot.

"You okay?"

"I am now!"

"Can you walk?"

"I'll crawl if I have to."

"Kitten," he said, feeling something twist in his chest. God, she was incredible. So brave. "I'm gonna spank your ass the second we're in a safe place."

"Can we discuss this later?" She sounded testy, a little sarcasm creeping into her tone.

She was alive. His chest constricted at the idea of losing her. His arms tightened around her damp body. Not gonna happen.

He ran from the clearing, relieved when he didn't hear them following. They would, he knew, because that's what he'd do once he'd regained his equilibrium. It was clear they'd never seen a shifter before. They'd reminded him of primitive tribes on ancient Earth, the ones he'd learned about at school.

Sweet baby Jesus, who cooked people in a pot? Eva was lucky his gut instinct had told him to return, that something was wrong. When he'd found Bluebird alone, looking for her too, he'd started to worry.

A soft, inquiring honk came from the bushes.

Bluebird.

Saber kept running, eyes scanning the undergrowth for a hiding place. The bird scuttled past him in a burst of speed and darted down a path to the right. Saber slowed, glanced over his shoulder and saw they hadn't caught up yet, and picked his way through the grasses and past the bushes to alleviate signs of his passing. He'd leave Eva in a safe place and lay a false trail to make doubly sure the tribe didn't find them.

Bluebird led him to a hollow pink tree trunk and after checking inside, he set Eva down.

"Where are you going?" Tension pulled at her pinked arms and shoulders while her blue eyes went wide, a little wild.

He brushed her hair from her face and trailed his fingers over her cheek. He smiled even though the bright-pink patches on her skin concerned him. "I'm not leaving you for long. Let me untie you."

Saber made short work of her bonds and took care not to hurt her as he checked for injuries. "Are you okay?"

"My skin is tight, a bit sore."

"Rest here. I'll be back soon."

"No! Don't leave me!"

"Quiet, they'll be looking for us. I want to lay a trail for them to follow, one that leads them away from here. If you stay quiet, you'll be safe."

A soft honk at his back made Saber smile. Bluebird was weird in appearance, reminding him of an ungainly dodo bird with a bit of goose thrown in. Not the prettiest creature, but he was one kickass security bird.

Eva bit her lip, her eyes filling with a sheen that foretold tears. Understandable, given her recent ordeal.

"I'll be back as soon as I can."

A tear tumbled down her cheek and she ducked her head. Saber's heart turned over. He wanted to scoop her into his arms and comfort her, never let her go.

He stood abruptly and shifted to feline. After one quick scent of the air, he moved away from Eva, even though his heart protested with every prowling step.

CHAPTER EIGHT

N ow that she found herself safe, tears rolled down Eva's cheeks and refused to stop, no matter how hard she willed otherwise. Her skin felt dry, tight and hot, and sweat poured off her, between her breasts and in other uncomfortable places.

She tried not to think about the alone part, the roaming tribesmen, the big-ass birds, the ribbons of moving fire and the fact that she was on Tiraq instead of Dalcon.

But the tears kept coming, her throat aching.

Frying fungus. Time was running out and they seemed no closer to the resort. Every dangerous situation she stumbled into just delayed them further.

She'd never get rid of the Dearbhorgaills.

She'd never avenge Pryce's death.

She'd failed.

Once he'd checked things out and made an obvious trail in human form for the cannibals to follow, Saber shifted back to cat and went to find them. They were following the false trail, although it was apparent the underlings weren't enthusiastic. Their steps lagged, and the one at the front barked commands to hurry them along.

Saber slipped noiselessly through the undergrowth until he was ahead of them before letting out a hair-raising shriek. The jungle went quiet, and Saber snickered silently. He crept back to where the cannibals stood, frozen in position.

The obvious leader, a tall dude with a bone threaded through his nose, gave a sharp order. The troop moved again, but the ones at the rear twisted their heads around, surveying every inch of the tangled profusion of plants surrounding them.

Saber smirked and let rip with another feral feline scream. The troop jumped, and two at the back broke ranks.

How many roars would it take to break the leader?

Saber slunk closer until he was almost level with Bone Nose and let rip.

The blue-faced man leaped a foot in the air, gave a high-pitched screech, and turned in the direction of their camp, almost knocking down the rest of the troop in his race for safety. When they'd all picked themselves up and scuttled in the direction of the camp, Saber gave a feline grunt of satisfaction. Only three. No challenge at all.

He checked the trail for signs of danger then made a quick detour to a sandy desert area he'd discovered earlier. Things to do. Places to go.

A mischievous woman to deal with.

When he arrived back at the tree where he'd left Eva, Saber had been half expecting to find her gone. To his relief, she'd stayed and was now asleep. When he crept closer, he saw she'd been crying, the dried tracks of tears staining her cheeks. Regret surged through him and tightened his chest.

This was his fault, yet if he were honest, he wouldn't do things differently.

He set down the fruit and the plants he'd been carrying and absently petted Bluebird when the creature pressed up against his side.

"Eva, wake up." He shook her shoulder, ready to slap his hand across her mouth should he startle her. "Wake up, kitten."

He had to talk to her, persuade her not to run away again because it wasn't safe.

Then another thought occurred. Maybe his dual nature scared her. She hadn't acted with distaste, but maybe...

She didn't give away much in her expressions, not unless she wanted to, and pasted on emotions with deliberation.

"Kitten."

Her eyelids fluttered, and she came awake, her muscles going tense.

"It's me," he murmured. "They've returned to their village. I don't think they'll be bothering us again. Are you hungry?"

She shuddered. "I can't think of food now, not when I-I..." She trailed off, a violent tremor spearing through her body.

"We'll save it for later. How is your skin? You're lucky they put you in, clothes and all."

"I don't think they'd worked out that they came off. They probably thought to...ah...remove them later." Another tremor shook her slight frame at the idea of being the dish of the day for cannibals.

"Think on the bright side. At least you don't have to walk buck-ass naked through the jungle."

Her brow wrinkled, but she pushed hard for humor. "And my clothes are clean." She didn't quite pull it off, although he gave a faint grin and ran a gentle hand over her head.

"Let me check your feet. I have a plant that might help ease your burns." He removed her socks and hung them on a branch. "Lift your T-shirt. Ah, it's not too bad. Your skin is a little pink." He broke the long leaves and spread the thick sap within over the pinked skin with gentle fingers.

The tension bled from her muscles until she lay relaxed in front of him. He doctored her then replaced her socks and shirt. "We need to move. By my reckoning it should take us another two days to reach the mining village. We'll be able to get transport from there."

She nodded.

"I'll carry you—at least until it becomes too dark to travel."

"I can walk."

"Kitten, you'll slow us down. I can make better time carrying you."

"What was that stuff you put on my skin?"

"I don't know what it's called here, but the plant looks like aloe, one we had on Earth."

"The advertising for the resort mentions that most of the employees are from Earth. Why did you leave?"

"A virus was killing off our species. There were many deaths...including my fiancée, Lori." Saber was quiet for a few long, painful moments. "After that, we decided to leave and find a new home where we'd be safe." He lifted her into his arms, deciding to carry her in front of him, even though it was more awkward. Piggyback style was practical, but given her injuries, he thought this way would work best. Bluebird would alert them to any dangers.

"I'm sorry for your loss," she said quietly. She sighed. "So...which way are we going?"

"A process of elimination. The cannibal troop is that way. The lava trail extends all the way down the side of the volcano. There's another in the direction I went this morning, so we need to go into the jungle again."

"The lava is on the other side of the village too."

"Then jungle it is," Saber said.

Full darkness had descended when he decided to halt for the night. He stopped by a patch of ferns, checked them for safety, and made a quick bed.

"How are you feeling?"

"Much better," she said.

"Do you want some fruit?"

At her nod, he handed her a red apple-like fruit and one that seemed cousin to an Earth banana, despite its vivid pink color.

"I need to reapply the plant juice," he said.

She nodded again, and her quietness disturbed him. He preferred her sassy insults, her quick mind, and even her escape attempts to this silence.

He tended to her and decided to do a quick reconnoiter before he rested. He stood and took only a few steps before Eva stopped him.

"Wait! Where are you going?"

"I want to check the vicinity and ensure there isn't anything dangerous in the area. I can hear water. If it's safe to drink, I'll bring some back for you."

"You won't be long?"

"I won't be long," he promised.

Eva started at every creepy jungle noise, and there were many of them. Give her the marketplace with its thieves and vagabonds any day. She could cope with the dangers in the market and was used to them even if they sometimes scared her. But this? In this place, a different danger lurked behind every tree and bush. Weird creatures. Enormous creatures. Hungry creatures.

Way too many beasties for her peace of mind.

At this point, she was only alive because of Saber. True, it was his fault she was in this situation to begin with, but he'd tried to keep her safe. The big bird would've eaten her the first day if it weren't for him. One of the big birds.

Beside her, Bluebird gave a whispery snore, and she petted him, comforted slightly by the creature's presence. But she was still wide awake and mostly terrified when Saber returned. One moment, he wasn't there, and the next, he was. She jolted, almost letting loose a screech of terror.

"Kitten, it's me. It's all right," he crooned, his hand sliding over her head in a gesture of comfort.

He was petting her again like she was Bluebird. The tension bled from her muscles. It felt good. Safe. "Sorry. I'm a bit jumpy."

"Understandable. Want some water?"

"Please." He was still tending to her. The thought brought back the need to cry. No one had ever looked after her before. *Not even Pryce*, her traitorous mind added.

He held a makeshift vessel to her mouth, and the water was cool as it slid down her throat. "I'll take you to the waterhole in the morning," he said once she'd drunk her fill. "The cool water will help your skin, and you'll feel better after a wash."

"Thanks." Still looking after her—which didn't make sense if the Dearbhorgaills were responsible for her kidnapping.

Saber settled beside her, and she snuggled close to his warmth.

"Why are you so desperate to get back to Dalcon?"

Eva swallowed. She might as well tell him. She was having trouble deciding if he was good or bad, especially when he took such care to keep her alive. He'd saved her from Bone Nose. He could have left her to her fate.

"I grew up in the market and was lucky the people who looked after me were decent. Instead of working as a pickpocket, which I was lousy at, I toiled in a restaurant from an early age. I met Pryce at one of the market restaurants." She let out a sound that masqueraded as humor. "That's what the owners called it. The place was a single room with four rough tables and even rougher clientele. The saving grace was the food. The wife of the owner worked magic when she cooked, and she taught me."

Eva paused to marshal her thoughts, the darkness making it easier to tell her tale. "I'd worked there for several years, waiting tables and cooking. The owners let me sleep in the restaurant after hours. I was safer than I'd been as a child, and while the work was hard, I was happy.

"Pryce came into the restaurant one night. Although he'd dressed the same as our regular customers, he was different. His speech. His mannerisms. He stayed for hours, ordering and trying the entire range of dishes on our meager menu. When we were ready to close, he was still there. He asked to speak to the owners and offered to buy them out. He said he wanted to create a chain of restaurants, and they could continue running the place, but he'd want their help with the menus and food in the other restaurants. We were initially suspicious because he was obviously wealthy, but even *we* were shocked when we discovered he was the son of the Dearbhorgaill family. We thought he was playing us, but the deal he offered was too good to refuse."

"You grew close," Saber said.

"Apart from Casey, he was the only friend I had. He kept his word, and the new restaurant he opened became very successful. He improved the original restaurant and made us all wealthy. Pryce had such plans. His parents pretty much ignored him until he became rich in his own right. They arranged a marriage for him, but he refused to go through with it. When they wouldn't relent, he asked me to marry him. He said he loved me and had intended to court me properly, but marrying him quickly would both make him happy and get his parents off his back."

Eva paused, the quick slice of guilt a familiar one. Why couldn't she have loved him? Pryce had deserved more.

"He was your friend," Saber said. "I'm sure you wanted to help, and I bet you were loyal, never cheated on him."

"No, I never cheated on him. His parents tried to accuse me of infidelity, but he didn't believe them. He never believed anything they said about me. Pryce was a special man. He was also ambitious. He started negotiating to purchase a third restaurant. We had to organize a loan because it was a large-scale project."

Eva took a deep breath and sighed. "Before the documents were signed, Pryce was murdered in the market. They never caught the murdering bastard, but I know the Dearbhorgaills had something to do with his death. They told everyone it was because Pryce was wandering through the market at nightfall. That was a lie. No one in the market would touch him. He'd become one of us. He helped everyone. Brought us together in a way we'd never experienced before. He'd married me, yet he never expected me to change, to be anyone other than who I was."

"What about his family? I take it they've caused trouble since their son's death? It's in your tone."

"They tried to take his money and restaurants, but Pryce had prepared for that. Unbeknownst to me, he'd put everything in my name, and I was to be awarded full control should he die under mysterious circumstances."

"They didn't like that, I take it."

"No. They took me to court, but the judge tossed out their case. I wanted to complete the formalities on the new restaurant, but the bankers had *mislaid* the paperwork. We did new paperwork, and they rejected my loan. Every official banker refused to loan me money. I found a private facility willing to complete the loan, but despite my research before signing, I failed to discover the Dearbhorgaills owned the company."

"I bet they had fun informing you of the fact."

Eva recalled the smug, superior expressions on their upper-class faces and cringed. It hadn't been her best day. "The second loan payment is due next solar week. If I don't make the payment, I'll lose everything. Pryce worked so hard for those restaurants. All his sacrifices will be wasted."

"You worked hard too."

She shot Saber a swift glance. "I owed him." But it was the truth, she realized. She'd put all her energies into Pryce's vision. She'd discovered she had a head for business, the killer instincts that made for success—except when she'd signed that loan document. But she'd been worried, out of her mind with grief. She still missed Pryce. His intelligent mind. His ready smile and good humor. His friendship and the way he listened to everything she said.

"I'll make sure you get to Dalcon," Saber said. "Two or three days should see us back at the resort. We'll fly to Dalcon and take care of your business. Do you have the money to make the payment?"

Eva chewed on her lip and considered lying. No. She'd tell him everything. "I have the money, but when I knew I was leaving Dalcon for a few days, I...I set a trap. The Dearbhorgaills have done everything possible to disrupt restaurant operations. My staff members quit without warning, my stock shipments go missing. We have break-ins. So many problems."

"Do you think your trap will work?"

"I hope so. It's not long until the third and final payment is also due. With all the disruptions, it might prove difficult to make the payment."

"And if you can establish the Dearbhorgaills are behind the problems?"

"It might make a difference. As long as the law and judge aren't in the Dearbhorgaills' pocket."

"I think we can work around that," Saber said. "They won't expect you to have allies. Go to sleep now. We have a couple of long days ahead of us." He pressed a kiss to her temple even as her eyes fluttered closed.

He believes me. That was her last thought as she tumbled into sleep.

"Wake up, kitten."

"Saber?"

"I'm here. Are you ready to go? How are you feeling?"

Eva stirred, pushing to her feet. The skin on her arms and legs was still faintly pink and a little sensitive, but other than that, she felt fine. "I was lucky you came."

Instead of answering, he leaned over, closing the distance between them to press his lips to hers. A slow, sensual nibble later, she sighed. *Frying fungus*, he was good at kissing. Of their own volition, her hands curled around his neck, fingers tangling in his black hair to hold him in position.

He lifted his head, stared at her with his green eyes, then he confounded her by pressing his forehead to hers and rubbing their noses together. The tender action made her heart pitter-patter, and she issued a lustful sigh. They didn't have time—she knew it—but she wanted him with an intensity that wouldn't stop.

"We'd better go," he repeated. He pulled back but reached for her hand, curled her fingers in his, and started walking.

She followed, reveling in the intimacy, so innocent, yet it made her heart race, her blood roar like a Salim banshee. Her breasts tingled, and a whoosh of sensations converged in her pussy. She'd never experienced that for Pryce.

An arrow of guilt struck center-front. Her grip tightened on his fingers, and he cast a quick look in her direction.

"Something wrong? Do you need me to carry you?"

"No, I'm fine." The man kept giving. He hadn't lost his temper with her even though, in hindsight, she'd behaved stupidly and put them both in danger.

The jungle around them was alive with sounds and life. She caught the occasional flicker of tiny furry creatures dangling from upper branches and others swinging from tree to tree. A group of golden-colored birds with bright-red beaks squabbled over meg-fruits, a type of spicy fruit with white flesh. She yanked on Saber's hand and grabbed a couple. Along with appeasing her hunger, they'd freshen her mouth. She hadn't considered the state of her breath when she'd kissed Saber earlier. Too shocked by the emotions coursing through her mind and body.

"These taste good. Luckily, I'm with a food expert. I wouldn't have known which were safe to eat."

"I believe a lot of the fruit on Dalcon is imported from Tiraq."

"Is it now? Maybe we should look at growing fruit as well as vegetables. Could you help us with that?"

"Of course," Eva said, her ready reply shocking her. Dalcon was her home, the sole refuge she'd ever known. Apart from a quick break after she'd married Pryce, she hadn't left Dalcon until Casey surprised her with this holiday.

Saber's smile was white and bright against his tan, his obvious approval lighting his green eyes. She gazed at his handsome face, and it dawned on her that he hadn't sprouted whiskers since they'd been away.

"You don't have a beard."

"I use stop-beard. Applied some not long before we left."

"Or other places." She made a quick gesture with her hand in the direction of his groin.

His grin turned toothy. "I didn't think you'd noticed."

"I noticed."

He came to a halt by a pool of water. "This is it. I've checked it for nasties. There's nothing in there to harm you, not even any of those fish." His eyes twinkled. "Anything else you want to ask?"

"Do your women have litters?"

He barked out a laugh. "Multiple births aren't uncommon. Mostly twins and occasionally triplets, but never more than that."

"And are they like you?"

"All shifter offspring are born with the ability to shift. In recent years, not all have survived the first shift—at least they didn't until we discovered diet plays a big part in making sure the right hormones are present. Too much sugar isn't a good thing."

Eva nodded, wanting to ask more questions but deciding to leave her queries until they stopped for the night again. During the day, they needed to go as fast as they could.

As if he could read her thoughts, he said, "We'd better have our swim and get moving. Want me to wash your back?"

Her gaze narrowed. Washing backs led to other things. "I thought you were in a hurry. We *are* in a hurry."

"We can spare an extra ten minutes. A quickie," he added, humor lurking in his pretty eyes.

He hadn't smiled much when she'd first seen him. A shame when he wore smiles and grins with such a rakish air.

"Take off your shirt."

"What's left of it," she murmured, already following his order.

"I'm enjoying the glimpses of your breasts."

"Oh." A compliment. She wasn't sure what to do with it. She threw the shirt into the water but left her socks hanging over a bush.

Saber dived into the pool and surfaced, droplets of water sparkling on his face. "Feels good."

It did, the water cool against her skin. She sighed and started washing herself. Such a pretty spot with the morning solar light and the tiny clearing, the sparkle of the jade-green water. It would be so easy to laze away the hours here.

Saber splashed, attracting her attention. "Come here," he said. "I promised to wash your back."

"You could fuck me too."

Her blunt words appeared to startle him.

"Maybe you were expecting a battle to get me to agree? I'm past that now," she explained. "You make me feel good. Sometimes very, very good."

He rubbed his chin. "Very, very good, huh? I'll strive for excellent."

She laughed, more at herself than him—because in that moment, she realized she was falling for him. This constant upheaval of her emotions—

No!

She didn't love him. She couldn't. It wasn't possible, not when her life was on Dalcon and his was here on Tiraq.

"Eva? Kitten?" His gaze was quizzical.

"Nothing." She wrapped her arms around his neck and pressed closer. His cock thrust out, ready to take her, ready to give her the pleasure she'd come to crave.

She wrapped her legs around his waist, opened herself to his touch, and he didn't disappoint her. Nimble fingers delved, rubbed, teased.

"Does that hurt?"

"No, my legs were the worst. I kept trying to jump out of the pot."

"Good job," he said. "Never make it easy for the enemy. Never give up. Never say die."

"We think the same way."

"We do," he said, the cocksure smirk one of male victory.

"Rub me right there," she demanded.

His finger slid over her clit, a smooth massage, her hot flesh a contrast to the temperature of the water surrounding their bodies.

"What about here?" He slipped a finger inside her and rubbed a bit of flesh. She shuddered, closed her eyes, cried out and came instantly around his finger.

"Beautiful," Saber said.

She opened her eyes to find him smiling at her.

"Let's do that again before we get moving." He held her tightly while piercing her with his cock.

He stretched her in a delightful way, filling then cradling her body while he did all the work. He drove up, thrusting and retreating. So, so good. Perfect. The threads of pleasure started to wind through her body again, twisting and turning until they knit into a huge ball. She reached down to touch her achy flesh and rubbed hard.

"Good, kitten. Take what you need."

Her finger froze. She hadn't even considered what he might think. She was so used to taking care of herself that she naturally—

"Don't stop," he ordered. "I enjoy watching you, feeling your fingers against my cock."

"B-but..."

"Nothing you do is wrong, kitten. Touch me, touch yourself," he whispered, his breath hot against her neck.

He received pleasure from being with her, and she...she liked him way too much for peace of mind. A recipe for a *freakin' fungus* of a disaster.

His thrusts were faster now. Harder. He groaned, the sounds close to a catlike purr. He kissed her skin, lightly nipped at the spot where shoulder met neck.

His teeth. They seemed sharper, longer...

"Ready to come for me, kitten?"

Eva rubbed her clit furiously, the stirrings of pleasure pushed to prominence by his sexy voice. *Frying fungus*, she loved his voice, his body.

She exploded, her fingers digging into his shoulder for purchase as he slammed into her. Once, twice. On the third hard plunge, he stayed planted deep, and she felt the contractions of his cock as he came.

Saber lowered his head and kissed her. Their lips brushed in lazy unison. A slow and thorough kiss that sizzled clear to her toes.

"We'd better head out."

"I'll just give my shirt a quick scrub before I put it back on."

A short while later, Saber rubbed the gooey plant substance on the worst spots on her arms, legs and feet, then she dressed—as much as one could in a shirt and socks—and they set out on another long, exhausting walk.

The next day followed in a similar fashion. They walked and walked and walked, the only variable being the scenery and the colors of the plants and creatures. Bluebird followed them, sometimes going off to graze but always returning to spend the night by their side.

During the highest heat of the day, they rested and had slow, sweaty sex. They ate different types of fruit and once, Saber left her to go hunting for meat. She didn't partake of the feast.

Now evening was drawing in once more and they were looking for a safe place to spend the night.

"Are those buildings?" Eva asked, pointing at a hill.

Saber looked in the direction she indicated. "Looks like ruins. Maybe a deserted village. Want to check it out?"

"It might work for tonight's camp."

Nodding agreeably, Saber reached for her hand and headed for the hill.

"It does look deserted," Eva said once they stood in the middle of the ruins. "I wonder what happened to the residents."

"Maybe the birds got them. The plains would make for easy hunting."

"Don't tell me that."

"Don't worry." Saber studied the plains below and pointed to a sliver of jade green in the distance. "Look. That's the coast. We're almost there. If we leave early tomorrow, we should manage to reach it before the thermals make it easier for the birds to fly. We'll get you back to Dalcon."

In the face of such confidence, she wasn't going to argue. He hadn't failed her yet. "Thank you," Eva said.

"Now—which one?" He gestured to the buildings, many of which were collapsed by trees or had bushes growing inside them.

She and Saber wandered around the different dwellings then rounded a corner. One building stood in the center of what would have once been an open square. Now a profusion of colorful flowers filled the space around it, but the building appeared intact.

"That's weird. Stay here while I check it out."

Bluebird honked, one of an inquiring nature.

"I don't know," Eva said. "Oh look. There's an opal tree. The fruit is so expensive. She picked several before returning to the spot where Saber had left her.

His face sported a frown upon his return.

"Is it terrible inside?"

"No. Come and see."

He took her hand—a habit she was coming to enjoy—and led her around the building and inside.

"It smells as if the owners have been gone for a while."

Eva gaped at the luxurious ruby syn-silk fabric covering the low sleep-bed, the gold and ruby pillows, a tray of food and drink, the cool cube with its solar light indicating it was on and cooling the contents. A hot cube. A nook in which to eat.

This was so much like the poor-girl dreams she used to have when she slept rough on the streets, before she started working at the restaurant in the market.

There was even a small med-box. Maybe she could apply healing salve to her myriads cuts, bruises and burns. She opened a door and found a luxurious cleansing room and another offshoot, which appeared full of clothes. Some glamorous and others more practical. And footwear!

"It has a sanitizer! And clothes. Clothes that would fit me. Do you think these people would have transport? We could pay them to take us to the resort. I wonder where they are."

"I checked the other buildings. They're all ruins. Derelict."

"Do you think the residents will return tonight?"

"There's no scent trail—either in or out of the building. It's as if someone put the stuff here and transported back out with a travel-beam."

"What about inside? Is there a scent here or maybe in the cleansing room?"

"Nothing."

Eva stared at him, her frown echoing his scowl. "That's a little peculiar. What should we do?" A part of her realized she was asking his advice instead of acting independently, as was her normal manner.

Saber's brows rose, almost as if he were reading her mind. He gave her a quick flash of grin and her lower belly—and her pussy—pulled tight. Whether in alarm or desire, she decided she wouldn't examine her response too closely.

"What do *you* want to do?" he asked in a silky voice.

CHAPTER NINE

E va didn't break his gaze. "*I* want to strip off what's left of this shirt, the socks, and jump into their sanitizer. Once I'm squeaky clean, I'll treat my injuries and eat some of their food and drink. Then, tomorrow, if our gracious hosts haven't returned, I suggest we leave an IOU for the hospitality. Now you."

"I'm up for your plan, as long as it includes bed and some hot sex." Saber smiled again, the green color of his eyes so pretty in his masculine face, she stared harder. It was like dropping into freefall.

Sexy and brutal.

A little scary.

Liberating.

A laugh started to build deep in her gut. It exploded from her throat in a sound of pure joy. "Last one in the sanitizer is a rotten stink egg." She sprinted for the cleansing room, and once she was through the door, she flung off her shirt and stooped to roll off her socks. They landed with a plop on the tiled floor.

Saber was right behind her, his boots already hitting the floor. He grabbed her by the shoulders before she slipped into the sanitizer and hauled her around to face him. His eyes were even greener than normal, and she giggled—actually giggled—the carefree sound astonishing her. She ceased her struggles and let him draw her close.

He licked a slow line down her neck, his tongue rough against her tender skin. On the return erotic journey, he stopped near her ear. "A cat loves to stalk its prey," he whispered.

His hot breath sent a shudder through her. She wasn't sure how to take his murmured words. A threat? A promise? "Is that a good thing?"

"It is if there's sex involved." He used his finger to tip up her chin and placed a gentle kiss on her upturned lips. "Do you trust me, Eva? Will there be sex?"

"Yes." Heat bloomed in her cheeks when she realized she hadn't hesitated.

Saber reached past her to power up the sanitizer. "In you go." He gave her a gentle shunt and crowded in behind her before closing the door of the unit.

"I don't think—"

Saber's mouth came down on hers. This time his kiss was hard, almost savage. His arms were tight around her, and she felt the pressure of his rigid length against her belly. His tongue slid into her mouth and dueled with hers. He ravaged her mouth, his hands wandering, teasing, a little groping and lots of stroking while the sanitizer performed its wash, rinse and dry cycles.

When he opened the door to the unit and let them out, she felt sparkly clean, and her knees worked like limp noodles. She staggered, and Saber chuckled.

"Food, I think." He plucked her off her feet and carried her over to the platform sleep-bed in the other room. "But there's something else we need to deal with first."

"What?" Eva pushed her befuddled mind and gave it a swift mental kick to help it reset. Clear as Dalcon mud. "Oh, you mean the medi-box. It's over there."

Saber sat on the edge of the bed and, in one quick move, had her facedown and draped over his knee.

"What are you doing?" Eva attempted to scramble off, but he held her easily.

"Giving you the spanking you deserve for scaring the fuckin' crap out of me," he said in a matter-of-fact voice.

His hand came down hard on her buttocks. The sting shocked her, paralyzed her mind again. The second blow dragged a yelp from her throat.

"Stop! You can't smack me! I'm not a child."

The third blow came, and *frying fungus*, it hurt.

"You acted like a child." *Smack.* "You put yourself in danger." *Smack.* "I probably have gray hair sprouting as we speak." *Smack.*

Oh, *flibbergidgit*, that hurt.

Smack.

He shifted her slightly, changed the angle of the blow. It still hurt—but a surprising jolt of heat went through her. While she was considering that, he struck her again. Another different angle.

Flying Finnian bats. Along with the slap of pain came another arrow of heat.

"Nothing more to say?" he taunted. "No more excuses?" He punctuated his words with sharp slaps.

"I thought you were in league with the Dearbhorgaills."

Smack. "I've never met them."

"They could have hired you through a third party."

Smack. Smack. "I am *not* an assassin for hire." *Smack. Smack.*

Now she'd done it. Her poor bottom smarted. It was hot and tender while her pussy ached with an echo of her pain. She didn't understand her body's reactions one bit.

"Anything else you want to say?" he asked, his voice silky.

"Uh…" Her brain had gone blissfully blank, and all she could think of was the next blow on her bottom. Would it hurt again? Or would it ratchet up the ache between her thighs?

"Eva?"

There was clear warning in his testy tone. What did he want her to do? Her brain struggled to formulate a reply even as he spanked her again. The pain arced over her buttocks and to her needy core. Without thinking, she raised her buttocks.

Saber gave a hard laugh. "Eva?"

He wanted her to do something, but what? He was angry because she'd run away, caused him to worry, and had almost died in the cooking pot. She got that. In hindsight, she hadn't acted wisely, but he'd kidnapped her. What was she meant to think?

Smack.

Tears sprang to her eyes, a direct contrast to the edgy sensation, the almost pleasurable sensation that tingled in her pussy.

"Eva?"

Finally, *finally* something clicked in her mind.

Frying fungus. He wanted her to apologize.

Smack.

"*Ow*, I'm sorry. Is that what you want to hear? Do you think I enjoyed being an ingredient in a stew? It wasn't my idea of a fun day out. My birthday, and one I'll never forget."

"Your birthday?"

"Yes, well, the day I celebrate. I don't know the real date of my birth."

His hand settled on the hot skin of her buttocks and stroked. "Not the most gracious apology I've ever heard." An odd note colored his tone. "But I guess it will do."

He turned her over, and her gaze went straight to his face. The horrid man was trying not to laugh.

"It's not funny."

His humor slipped away. "That's my point. I was worried about you. If I'd arrived twenty minutes later, you'd have been dead."

Contriteness bloomed inside her. "I know. I'm sorry."

"Don't do it again. Talk to me," Saber said. "Know that I will never hurt you intentionally." He lifted her and placed her facedown on the bed. "Stay there, and I'll get the medi-box."

She sank into the mattress, her backside aching, her pussy aching, her feet aching. A fair portion of her body throbbed now that she thought about it.

Saber returned to her side and sat. He opened the medi-box and grunted. "They have the good stuff. Expensive."

The cooling touch of the gel on her backside made her groan in appreciation. "That feels so good." Already the tightness and heat were retreating, the tiny healing nanos in the gel doing their work.

Saber rubbed the gel into bruises, cuts, and the lingering spots caused by hot water. He treated the backs of her legs and her feet. "Turn over for me."

Eva rolled, feeling more relaxed than she had since leaving the resort. Saber continued to minister to her until all the achy pain left her body. "Would you like me to do you?"

"Later." Saber grinned. "After food. My stomach feels as if my throat has been cut."

"Charming."

"What do you want to eat?"

"I don't mind. Anything, as long as it's filling."

Eva watched Saber rub the healing gel on his body, but he didn't have many ouchies. She stared openly, allowing herself the thorough visual tour she hadn't before. He had a strong body, a fit one with sculpted pecs and ridges that went down his belly. His cock thrust out in an impudent manner, the ruddy head glistening. Someone was thinking about sex.

Someone else, she amended silently. That was her one remaining ache—a sensual one that seemed to bloom and grow with every lingering peek at his hot body.

"I should move," she said.

"Stay there. Let me get you something to eat and drink."

Saber wandered over to the cool cube. Her mouth watered at the idea of a decent meal. While she enjoyed fruit, she didn't want to eat it for days on end. She thought about her favorite dish, with hot spices and vegetables and noodles. *Frying fungus*, she could practically smell the fragrant spices cooking.

"Drink this," Saber said, handing her a glass of water. "You're dehydrated. We should have drank water as soon as we arrived."

She downed the liquid. "What are you cooking in the hot cube?"

"I don't know. I picked a meal and put it inside to heat." A ding signaled the end of cooking, and Saber went to retrieve it. "Take a seat, and I'll serve your meal."

Eva glanced down at her naked body. "I'll grab a robe first. I'm sure I saw one in the other room. Do you want one?"

"Why not?" he said. "Let's do formal and dress."

Eva grinned at his casual ease with his nakedness. "Just because you and your people go around naked doesn't mean I need to follow suit."

"But the scenery is so pretty."

He actually meant that. It gave him pleasure to look at her. No one, not even Pryce, had complimented her on her appearance. The closest she ever came was "scrawny", and she was even leaner at present. She plucked a turquoise robe off a hanger and rifled through the clothes until she came upon a green one, just a fraction lighter than Saber's eyes. Perfect.

Robe donned, she ambled back to Saber, her limbs, her breasts becoming heavy under his close scrutiny.

"Very pretty," he said, his gaze drifting down her body, garbed in the form-fitting robe. "Have a seat. Dinner is served." He gestured at the table.

"That's my favorite meal!" she said.

"Mine too," Saber said, indicating a plate with a big steak. "Want some beer, or would you prefer wine? They have a bottle of wine from Earth."

"I'd love some," she said, her stomach gurgling in anticipation. "I can't wait. I have to taste this."

Saber settled opposite and handed her a glass of the wine. "No need to wait."

The taste of the familiar spices danced across her tongue. The vegetables were cooked but still crisp, while the noodles were better than any she served in her restaurants. She swallowed and groaned. "That is delicious."

"My meal is good too," Saber said after swallowing a mouthful of meat. He cut open a food she hadn't seen before. It was white inside and had a crispy skin. He added a thick, creamy substance and a knob of butter to the white part and sprinkled on a chopped green herby plant. "Vegetable," he said with a lazy smirk.

Oh, my fruity starters. She wanted to eat *him.* The sex part of his equation was looking better and better. The ache in her pussy, the throb in her breasts—they were transmitting urgent communications to the rest of her body. She lowered her gaze and stared at the cooling vegetables on her plate.

"Eat up," he said. "You're going to need your energy."

She jerked her gaze up and got lost in those incredible eyes of his. Way too easy to imagine waking up to those every solar day. Way too easy. This path of thinking—it wasn't good for her.

Enjoy, the logical part of her brain whispered.

Enjoy, the temptress inside her crooned.

Enjoy.

"Do you like the wine?"

Eva started and his brows lifted, silent humor dancing in his gaze. She grasped the glass and took a swig.

"Hey, that wine costs a bomb on Earth. I imagine with import taxes that it costs a small fortune here. Sip. Savor."

"Ah, sorry." He was right of course. She took a sip and let the liquid sit on her tongue before swallowing. Hints of tropical fruits, sunshine. Delicious. "It's good."

"Do you think we should attempt to make some here?"

"You know how?"

"My family owned vineyards on Earth. We all know how to make wine. It's a matter of growing the vines. We have some in stasis, along with several other Earth plants, and could import more at a price. The soil looks suitable."

"You should make wine," she said. "Make it exclusive to your resort and charge a premium for it. Play the nob factor."

"Nob?"

"One who thinks they're better than anyone else and expects to have the best, and shoves the lower levels' noses in the fact they can afford luxuries."

"Ah," he said. "I like it."

Feeling less jumpy, she set about demolishing her meal. Saber did the same, and her hunger subsided for the first time in days.

"Dessert?" Saber asked.

"What do we have?"

"I'll surprise you." Saber removed their empty plates, poured her another glass of wine, and tipped up her chin to steal a kiss. She was still tingling all over when he swaggered to the cool cube and pulled out something white. When he set it in the middle of the table, she saw the top was studded with juicy red berries and something else resembling shards of syn-choc.

Saber sat at the table and cut into the dessert. "Pavlova. My favorite dessert." He slid a dish over to her and served a larger portion for himself. "It's crunchy on the outside with a fluffy center. The meringue is always covered with cream and decorated with strawberries, raspberries and blueberries, and slivers of dark chocolate. My mother used to make one for my birthday every year."

Clear pleasure shone on his face. Happy memories.

She didn't have many of those.

"Don't." Saber reached for her hand and laced their fingers together. "Life is what you make of it. In the future, you'll think of today and the pleasure we found in being clean and safe, eating our favorite foods, and drinking glasses of celebratory wine. When we think of pavlova, we'll both smile."

As always, his touch made her heart race, her world right. "Do you think your mother would give me the recipe?" She imagined making Saber's favorite dessert and presenting it to him on his birthday. If she had the recipe, she could experiment and find substitutes in order to make the dessert. She could—

Frying fungus. No point in imagining the future. They didn't have one. Not together.

"Yes, if I ask her. Try it." He cut into the hard outer shell with his spoon, scooped up a little of the topping and a glossy berry then held it out to her. "Open up."

Eva's heart beat a little faster, and her hot spots set to tingling again. She opened her mouth and closed it around the dessert, sliding it off the spoon. Sweetness from the white contrasted with the tart berry. She swallowed, her eyes sliding to half-mast while she cataloged the textures and flavors. "Delicious."

Saber gestured at her plate with his spoon. "Enjoy."

Not a problem. She set about demolishing her dessert, and finally, with her stomach full and happy, she set her spoon down and pushed her plate away. "Thank you."

Saber stood and held out his hand. With his other, he scooped up both their glasses of wine before leading her to the sleep-bed. He set the glasses down on a bedside unit.

"I want you now."

Eva sucked in a quick breath, not moving when he unfastened her robe and let it slide to the floor. It landed in a silky whoosh, but neither of them took their gazes off each other. Her belly quivered as his stare heated, his eyes lowering to study her mouth.

"I want to fuck that luscious mouth of yours," he whispered. "I want to suck your tits until your nipples stand out. And then I want to slide between your thighs and take you hard, go so deep you'll still feel me tomorrow. And most of all, I want to mark you with my scent so no one doubts to whom you belong."

"You mentioned the scent thing before." Heat collected in her cheeks at his words, but her mind fastened on the last part of his sensual statement. *Belong?* He wanted her to *belong* to him? "I—"

"No," he whispered. "No more talking." And he made sure she couldn't talk anymore by sealing his lips over hers.

CHAPTER TEN

S aber gloried in her, the way her arms wrapped around his neck and clung to him. She parted her lips and let him explore in the way he'd wanted ever since sliding the spoonful of pavlova into her mouth.

When he lifted his head, he was breathing hard. Urgency throbbed through his veins, propelling him to haste. He scooped her off her feet and settled her on the sleep-bed. Fuck, this was gonna be good. A real bed. Soft and clean. No imminent danger.

At the thought, he reconsidered. Best to check.

"I'll be back in a sec. I want to reconnoiter outside. Make sure everything looks normal before we fuck." He wanted to laugh at her deer-in-headlights expression. Nothing like a little bluntness to keep her quiet.

He stalked to the exit and opened the door, the silky robe fluttering around his legs. Darkness had fallen while they'd cleaned up and ate. Distant stars glittered in the sky. He cast out his senses for danger. Insects clicked in the trees. A bird squawked over to his left—not a cry of danger, so he ignored it.

A familiar honk came from nearby. Saber followed the honk and found a large dog-house type structure he hadn't noticed before—that perhaps hadn't *been there* before. Rustling sounds came from inside, plus another honk. At the opening sat a dish of water and another of grain. A blue head poked out the doorway, gave another honk, and retreated.

Saber straightened, frowning. "Interesting," he murmured, tossing over the events of the evening in his mind. The favorite foods. The fitted clothes. Everything they needed...even for Bluebird. "Curious."

Shrugging, he listened again, and when he heard nothing to disturb him, he strode inside and shut the door. He turned the lock, added a chair under the handle for extra security, and returned to Eva.

"Everything okay?"

"Nothing out of place," he said, dropping his robe on the floor. He crawled onto the bed and started to play. Pleasing himself simply by touching her, testing the areas that made her issue soft sounds of enjoyment.

"Saber."

"Love hearing my name on your lips, kitten." He clambered over her and straddled her hips. His hands wandered, shaping her breasts and flicking her nipples. "It's good to see your skin smooth and unblemished. I didn't enjoy seeing you hurt."

"I wasn't keen on it either." Her voice was husky and breathy, her blue eyes wide and brimming with heat.

He ran his fingertips over her lower lip, gave a gasp when she took one finger inside her mouth and sucked. The warmth she generated reverberated through his entire body, striking his groin with lashes of promise.

"Kitten," he whispered.

Her gaze went to his, and he felt himself swallow. Damn, this woman tangled him in knots. She was brave, so brave, and didn't bitch about her fatigue or injuries. And she'd had a shitload of them. He knew because he'd played doctor.

"Take my cock in your mouth." He pulled his fingertip away and repositioned his body. "I want to feel the same heat around my cock. Feel the slide of it against your tongue." As he spoke, he traced his dick around her lips. "Open."

She took him into her mouth, and the wet heat blew his mind. His dick was already primed, but this...this was almost too much sensation. His balls tightened to the point of pain as she prodded and licked the head of his cock. Good. So fuckin' good.

"Take me deeper," he ordered.

He shuddered when she complied with no hesitation. She pulled back and took him deep again.

"Can you taste me?"

She hummed around his tip, and he felt the buzz right to his balls. Unable to help himself, he cupped her face, holding her in place while he thrust.

When she made a choking sound, he pulled back. He rolled to his back and dragged her over him. With a firm hand at the back of her head, he encouraged her to recommence her ministrations.

She didn't disappoint, her gaze snaring his as she lowered her head. She ran her hand up and down his length then she sank her mouth over his cock head. Saber groaned, even though he'd watched her, known the exact moment he'd feel the heat of her mouth again. She explored with her lips, and his heart battered his ribs. A provocative flick of her tongue made him jump, and she laughed, even though her mouth was full of his dick.

"Hey, watch it," he said.

One of her blue eyes closed in a wink. His balls jolted. She slid the flat of her tongue over the underside of his cock. He shuddered with helpless pleasure, her slave and willing to do anything for her. She bobbed her head, taking him almost to the root, and a dark sound escaped him. It vibrated in his chest, and when she pulled up, he didn't think he could hold off much longer.

She sucked and pressed the tight surface between his balls with her fingertip. Just the right spot. He groaned and came hard, so hard he wondered if his brain was intact. He saw fuzzy shapes in front of his eyes, which cleared once he blinked. His muscles went limp like cooked noodles, and it was lucky he was lying on a bed. She swallowed him down, taking everything he had to give before lifting her head. A tiny bit of semen clung to the corner of her mouth, and it gave him another rush of pleasure.

A badge. A sign. His mark of possession.

"Kitten, that was better than my imagination. Thank you."

She grinned. "I enjoy having you in my power."

"Two-way street, kitten." Another fuzzy shape flickered behind Eva. Damn, she'd really done a number on him if he was still seeing things. A double blink cleared his vision, and her beautiful face came into focus.

Fuck, he never thought he'd be happy because a big bird toted him off and dropped him in the middle of nowhere.

He thumbed the speck of semen away and drew her down for a kiss. She tasted of him now. Triumphant, he felt a sense of achievement settling in his chest. Her soft sigh upped the satisfaction, the feeling she belonged to him. God, this woman...

She was so right for him on every level.

He thought about his brother, wondered fleetingly if Felix had changed his mind about his new choice of mate, and was perhaps disappointed Saber had flown off with his captive. Too late now. He didn't intend to give up Eva. He kissed her, tantalizingly brief kisses on her mouth, her nose, over each eyelid.

Sated, he no longer felt the need to rush. No, he intended to take his time, to seduce her until she quivered beneath his touch, desperate for the final culmination. His hands wandered her slight body.

"We've both lost weight," he said.

She gurgled, a short burst of amusement. "I'd put on weight while lazing around your resort. Casey kept plying me with fruity little drinks—the ones festooned with fruit and cute umbrellas—and lots of snacks. You know. The ones they call canapés."

"Ah, my mother," he said, a fond grin settling on his lips. "She wanted an Earth menu, even if room service or the waitresses in the restaurant have to explain the terms."

"The food is excellent. Do you think I can have some of those recipes too? I'd like to experiment in my kitchen at home and attempt to recreate the dishes."

Saber slid his mouth over hers to stop the outpouring of words. The resort was her home now, and he didn't intend to argue about it, nor bring up the topic now when there were more interesting things to do.

Her hands tightened on his shoulders and suddenly he didn't want to go slow any longer. He rolled, placing her body beneath him and settling in to feast on her mouth.

"God, I love kissing you. So sexy, kitten."

His hands wandered her breasts, held the soft weights and relearned their shapes. He plucked a nipple and teased them both until they were hard nubs. Only then did he take them in his mouth. He nipped and sucked until her tight grip told him she'd edged into frantic need.

"Saber." Her tone of demand confirmed her desire.

Her eyes were squeezed shut, her body straining beneath his. He didn't intend to let her move unless it suited him. Instead, he took quick nips at her tummy, soothed them with his tongue before moving lower.

"I want to see your pretty pussy."

He shifted down the bed, and she parted her legs for him, baring herself with full trust, and that undid him. He stared at her swollen pink flesh, the glistening juices that coated her folds. His heart pounded and did a kind of somersault. He swallowed hard and reached out, trailing one finger over the heart of her with delicate precision.

She shivered, and unable to resist, he bent his head to give her a firm lick. Her hands fastened in his hair, holding him in place with determined strength. Inwardly, he smiled, enjoying the show of bossiness as she attempted to guide his mouth where she wanted it most. She was comfortable with him. Her piquant taste exploded on his tongue, and he licked thoroughly because it was obvious she enjoyed his attentions.

Then he lifted his head, stared at the passion on her face, the color in her cheeks and her swollen lips, almost red rather than pink. "You look beautiful."

Her eyes snapped open, and she studied him. "No one has ever told me that before."

"Not lying, kitten. No reason to butter you up when I know you're a sure thing."

She wrinkled her nose, and he laughed, the sound still startling to his ears. Surprising. He hadn't laughed much since Lori had died.

"Even though I've lost weight?"

"Even though." He moved up to kiss her, slow, lingering, putting every one of his chaotic feelings into the exchange. He kissed her deeply, copping a feel of her breasts until she wriggled beneath him and her fingertips dug into his rump.

When he slipped between her legs and pushed home, she sighed—a throaty sound that lit his senses, shoved at his urgency. Her tight, wet flesh hugged him in an intimate embrace, and he held himself still, firmly planted to the root, her channel flexing around his girth.

Fuck. This is good. Perfect. Easy to imagine being right here for years.

Saber, the man, wanted her.

Saber the feline desired her.

He pulled back and pushed into her enticing heat. Watched her face, her eyes still closed as if she wanted to concentrate on every feeling, the color in her cheeks delightful.

His feline rolled under his skin, and urgency built in Saber until he couldn't keep up the slow pace any longer. Lust and love bubbled in him, filled him to capacity until even his heart ached.

His feline challenged his control, his teeth changing, his claws starting to protrude from the ends of his fingernails. Fuck. That had never happened before Eva. Thank god her eyes remained closed so she couldn't see.

His hips snapped, the drag of his flesh against hers fueling his desire, fueling his urgency, fueling his feline. Saber couldn't stop. He craved her heat, craved her touch. He plain craved Eva.

Saber slammed into her, lowered his head to lick her throat.

"Saber!" That fuckin' sexy, throaty voice again.

She was gonna be the death of him. His pulse raced, his senses working overtime, filling him with light and pleasure and happiness. His gaze hit the fleshy part where her neck and shoulder met, and his tongue flicked out to taste.

If he thought he'd felt urgency before, he'd been mistaken. His cock throbbed, the painful echo squeezing his balls while his skin tingled with a tightness he'd never experienced before.

He licked that fleshy spot. Back and forth. Back and forth. She groaned beneath him, her hips lifting to meet his hard strokes, fingertips biting into his flesh, holding him close. Wanting him. Needing him.

He licked her again, the taste of her exploding through her skin. Fragrant. Tasty.

His.

Saber bit down, his sharp teeth slicing effortlessly into her tender skin. She jerked beneath him, cried out, and her sheath rippled around his cock. As the taste of her blood exploded in his mouth, he came so hard he saw the flurry of fuzzy, ghostly shapes around him. He kept coming, and was aware of the rhythmic tightening of her pussy.

The ghostly shapes brushed his skin, and the longer he came, the more opaque the shapes appeared.

Saber blinked, but the white shapes remained, floating above and around their bodies. Strangely, he didn't feel fear. Instead, he felt intense peace. He lifted his head...

The sight of blood at her neck jolted him.

Fuck.

He'd bitten her.

He licked the blood away and watched, a little astonished, as the wound healed in front of him to leave a small black scar in the shape of a leaping leopard.

But...

He'd thought...

An old legend.

Eva stretched languorously, shifting beneath him, a smile on her lips and her eyes still closed.

Dazed, Saber withdrew from her body and pressed a tender kiss to her lips. He blinked again. Both the black leopard scar and the ghostly shapes remained.

And a third thing—his cock was hardened already to a painful state.

He had to have her.

Again.

Right now.

"Turn over, kitten. Up on your hands and knees. Eyes closed so you can concentrate on the sensations."

Please keep your eyes closed so the ghosts don't freak you out.

There were so many of them now that it felt as if they were curtained on a four-poster bed.

He helped her into position and ran his hand over her rounded buttocks. She wriggled her ass from side to side.

Saber laughed. "Keep still, or I'll spank you again."

"I'm not sure if I should admit this, but by the end, I enjoyed my punishment. It was meant to be punishment, right?" Her throaty voice gripped something inside him, pulled it tight.

"Punishment and pleasure," he said and stroked her pussy with his dick.

"Again? Already?"

"Must be the comfortable sleep-bed." He wondered for an instant if she'd turn and look at him, but to his relief, she remained with her head down in the position he'd placed her.

She chuckled. "I feel wonderful. Maybe it *is* the bed."

She hadn't mentioned her neck, yet she'd cried out when his teeth had bitten into her flesh. Saber tried to remember the legend, the things his father had told him as a teenager. He wished he'd listened harder instead of fidgeting like the embarrassed teen he'd been.

Saber moved over Eva until he was draped along her back. He guided his cock to her entrance and pushed into her in a seamless stroke. "You feel so good, kitten. I love fucking you."

"Feels good on my end too," she whispered.

He withdrew and thrust again in an easy plunge.

The white shapes floating around the bed took on a faint hue of color. No amount of blinking changed the fact that they were becoming more corporeal. Saber's gaze went to the tiny leopard at her neck. That hadn't disappeared either.

He pushed into her, thought he loved her new tattoo and gave in to the temptation to lick the black cat. She trembled hard, and her pussy tightened around his dick.

Holy fuck.

He repeated the lick, and she responded in the same way, massaging his cock internally.

He quickened his strokes until he was slamming into her. He licked the tattoo at her neck and slipped one hand between her legs to tease her clit. She came almost immediately. Saber groaned. Thrust into her for two hard strokes. Felt good. Too good.

He wanted to hold back his orgasm, hold on to this magical sensation thrumming through his veins. But his third thrust annihilated his brain, pushing him into a mind-blowing climax.

He gasped for breath, his pulse thundering in his head as he planted his weight firmly on her back.

The whisper of a sound had his eyes opening, and he saw a man sitting in a chair by the side of the bed, one knee crossed over the other while he nursed a glass of ruby wine.

"Something wrong?" Eva asked.

Saber moved off her quickly and drew her protectively into his embrace.

"What— *Frying fungus*," she muttered when her gaze hit the same spot as his.

The man—clothed like a male out of one of the old costume dramas his mother and sister enjoyed so much—lifted his glass in a silent salute. Then he smiled.

"Thank you," he said in a rich voice. An upper-class voice that also belonged in one of those bloody costume dramas.

When Saber started to speak, the man held up a hand. Saber shut his mouth and waited. No need to panic—not until the man threatened Eva. Then all bets were off.

"Thank you for gifting us with your sexual energy." He smacked his lips. "A very piquant flavor. Tasty."

"Who are you?" Eva asked.

Saber's arm tightened around her shoulders, but a sense of pride filled him. His woman was full of courage.

"We are an incorporeal race. For so long we have been starved of energy. So long," he said. "But you have gifted us well. We'll leave you in peace." The man lifted his glass in another salute, took a sip, and faded away before their eyes.

"Well, hell," Saber muttered, still staring at the empty chair.

"I wish he'd taken the chair with him. If I need to use the restrooms early in the morning, I might stub my toe."

No sooner had she said the words than the chair disappeared, a rich chuckle echoing in the air around them.

"Hell," Saber repeated. "Was that real?"

"If you're hallucinating, then so am I," Eva said, staring at the empty spot where both man and chair had been.

"They were all around us while we were making love," Saber said, his gaze turning to hers. His green eyes glowed eerily, yet she didn't fear for her safety. The ghostly man hadn't scared her either. Something had told her they had nothing to fear.

"And you didn't say anything?"

"I thought I was seeing things."

Eva yawned. "I need some sleep. Maybe this will make sense in solar light."

"I doubt it. This is some freaky shit," Saber said.

"You won't get any argument from me."

His quick smile warmed her all the way through. He tugged back the bed covers. "It's getting cool."

She slid under the clean coverings with a contented sigh, turning on her side and closing her eyes. Saber settled in behind her, his larger body feeling protective and safe. She fell asleep with a smile on her face.

"Wake up." An insistent voice whispered against her ear.

"Is it time to go?"

"Soon." Saber wriggled against her, and she felt the prod of his erection against her bottom.

"Tired. Start without me."

His dark chuckle pulled a sleepy smile from her. "I can do that."

His nimble fingers tugged and stroked, caressed, and teased until the hum of arousal heated her blood. He remained behind her, so they were stacked like two cooking spoons. He lifted her leg, rearranged her body a fraction, and slid inside her.

She was a little sore, but she still wanted him, her wetness allowing him to move with ease.

He kept his thrusts lazy, her climax building in an easy fashion. He nuzzled her neck and licked the spot where her neck ended and her shoulder began.

"Feels so good," she said, and when his rough tongue rasped across the spot again, she exploded.

Saber grunted, moved into her with deliberate plunges now, and came four thrusts later, the splash of his seed filling her with warmth.

He held her for long moments afterward, the caress of his hand both soothing and arousing. Protective. Yes, she loved how he made her feel safe.

"Hungry?"

"Yes," she said after a few seconds of thought. Her stomach rumbled, an emphatic agreement.

"Right." His lips quirked, the corners moving in an uptick of humor. "Stay there. I'll bring you something to eat."

He slipped out of her, the covers rustling while he climbed from the bed. She must have drifted off to sleep again because she woke to him shaking her shoulder.

"Hey, sleepyhead. Breakfast is served."

He waited until she sat up, her back against the headboard, before he handed her a tray.

"I made bacon and eggs and toast," he said.

He lifted a red teapot and poured amber liquid into a cup. He handed it to her and she accepted it with a smile.

"I'd never tried tea until I went to your resort."

"Another Earth tradition," he said with an easy smile. He'd dressed while she slept and wore a clean pair of tight black trews and a pale green shirt that made his eyes more noticeable. His hair was tied back, baring the hard angles of his face. Long, glossy black boots covered his feet, hitting him at knee level.

"Very sexy," she said.

"Eat your breakfast before it gets cold."

She took another sip of her tea and tucked into the food. "I must've been hungrier than I thought," she said minutes later, staring at the empty plate with wonder. She never ate this much, never had the time when she was hurrying to complete day-to-day tasks and overseeing her employees.

"It's a pity we don't have transport to travel the last bit to the resort," she said. "A small shuttle. Even a fly-mo would do me."

"Until you come nose-to-beak with another colossal bird," Saber said.

"True. One close encounter is enough for me. Seeing them glide through the sky is scary, even knowing they can't see me beneath the trees." Eva sighed. "So we walk."

"A skimmer would get us there," Saber said. "We could skim the contours of the land."

"A nice dream." Eva drank the last of her tea. "I suppose we should clean up and go."

"The place appears to be self-cleaning," Saber said. "The things we used at dinner were clean when I went to make breakfast."

"How?"

Saber shrugged. "I don't know. Our host has mysterious ways."

Eva hurried through a quick wash and dress, thrilled to find a pair of black trews to fit and a thin blue top, perfect for the heat.

She even found black boots, replicas of the laced ones she'd seen in a High Street shop years ago and hadn't been able to afford.

"I'm ready," she said, walking and twisting her hair into a braid at once. She checked the result in a mirror and frowned. There was a black mark on her neck. She leaned closer to the mirror.

"You look gorgeous, but I like you naked best."

"What's this?" She tapped the black mark, shivering the instant her fingertip touched her skin. It was a black cat—and it resembled the same species of feline as Saber.

Saber's face went passive, all expression wiping clean. He knew something.

She glanced in the mirror again and rubbed her fingers back and forth over the black cat. She gasped when a streak of pleasure darted from her shoulder and frisked her hot spots before settling between her legs.

Coincidence?

Probably since her mind constantly dwelled on sex and Saber.

She lifted her fingers away, noted the cessation of tingles, then stroked the cat again. She whirled to stare at Saber.

"What have you done to me?"

CHAPTER ELEVEN

"I haven't done anything to you," he said, but his gaze connected with hers for a fleeting second.

"Saber..."

"I don't know what that is or why it happened. We should leave before the solar star gets too high in the sky."

Eva shot him a swift look and decided she'd ask again later. He seemed off-balance and, having come to know him, that concerned her. "Let's go then."

They headed for the door, and it opened by itself. Eva came to an abrupt halt. Saber slid his arm around her waist, his silent reassurance easing the prickling flesh on her arms and legs.

"Thank you." The ghostly voice echoed from all corners of the room. "We are pleased. Visit again soon."

"Right," Saber said, and he urged her outside.

Bluebird appeared from inside a small house and gave a honk.

Eva bent to stroke his brilliant blue feathers before something caught her attention.

"Look," she whispered.

A shiny shuttle sat not far from the building they'd exited.

Eva walked closer, wonder and hope tightening her chest. "It's a two-man shuttle."

"They heard us talking."

"They did a lot more than eavesdrop," Eva said in a dry voice. "I felt them touching me while we were making...ah, having sex. I've never come so hard in all my life."

"Me neither," Saber said. "Let's go." He strode to the shuttle, not even hesitating when a door opened before he reached it. "We can fly to the resort."

Eva hurried after him and tried not to think about the where and the how of this situation. Thinking too hard would just freak her out.

After placing Bluebird at her feet, she strapped in beside Saber. When the engine purred to life, a sense of loss enveloped her. Revenge was within her grasp, so why didn't that give her satisfaction?

The shuttle lifted into the air, and Bluebird honked and trembled. Eva stroked his feathers, and the bird settled.

"You don't have to go to Dalcon with me," she said, her hand stroking over Bluebird's back.

"I'm going with you," Saber said. "Once you bring down your in-laws, we'll talk."

"Talk about what?"

"Later," he said.

Eva scowled out the window, watching but not registering the flash of the scenery far below the shuttle. He was back to bossy, remote Saber—the man she'd first glimpsed at the resort—and she didn't understand why.

"We'll get one of my brothers to return the shuttle once we arrive at the resort. We can take the resort shuttle."

She nodded, and an uncomfortable silence fell between the pair. Eva idly stroked Bluebird, her thoughts drifting from bad to worse. What if she were too late? What if Pryce's parents had done something to make her lose everything? She wouldn't put it past her in-laws. *Frying fungus*, this was so unfair. She'd worked too hard for everything to implode on her now.

Pryce's legacy weighed on her shoulders like a load of grain-flour.

Saber concentrated on flying the shuttle. His hands clenched the controls while he struggled to maintain his temper.

She thought she was going to walk away from here, from *him*. Didn't she understand how right they were together?

He tried to remember all parts of the legend, pushing aside the faint discomfort when thoughts of Lori flitted to his mind. He hadn't felt half of this compulsion with her, and that brought guilt. The past. This—Eva—was his future.

If he and Eva were mated, as he suspected, he wouldn't want any other woman. No other female would appease the longing, the need, the plain desperation he held for Eva.

Surely she'd felt how good they were together? Each time they touched, it was magical. She soothed him, settled him, made him feel whole in a way he hadn't experienced since leaving Earth.

Eva was *home*.

He shot her a glance and saw her averted profile.

Hell, this wasn't gonna be easy.

But no way, no fuckin' way, did he intend to let her walk. She was his, as much as he was hers.

The acknowledgment eased the tightness in his chest. He'd deal. He'd go to Dalcon with her, and once they'd sorted out her problems, he'd tell her of his suspicions about the mating and ask her if she'd consider returning to the resort with him. She could open restaurants to her heart's content on Tiraq. He didn't care if she worked or lazed by the pool each day, just as long as she shared his bed every night.

Finally, still in a pulsing silence, the resort came into view. Saber hadn't bothered contacting his family on the com-unit, but he did so now.

"Come in, Scarlett," he said in a brusque tone.

The reply was almost instantaneous. "Saber? Is that you? Where are you? Let me get Felix."

"No, Eva and I will arrive soon. Can you get Felix to prepare the shuttle? Eva and I need to go to Dalcon."

"Dalcon? But I thought you'd—"

"Over and out." Saber cut in before she blabbed anything about the chase. He wanted to tell Eva the truth in his own time. Hearing a patchy explanation from his sister would complicate matters more than they were already.

Saber landed the craft on the shuttle pad. Felix was waiting for him.

"Where the hell have you been?" Felix demanded. "Are you both okay?" His gaze landed on Bluebird. "What the hell is that?"

"Is the shuttle fueled?" Saber saw Laurence skulking in the background. Lori's twin was an odd man.

"Yeah," Felix said. "I got Laurence to take care of that for you."

"Thanks. We'd better go. I need someone to return this shuttle." Saber plucked Bluebird from Eva's arms and handed the honking bird to Felix. "This is Bluebird. Give him to Scarlett to look after."

"It's not dinner?" Felix asked.

"Bluebird is *not* dinner," Eva snapped. "And if I come back and discover Bluebird missing, I'll hunt you down."

Saber caught the quirk of his brother's lips, quickly controlled, and grinned. *His woman.*

"Yes, ma'am." Felix turned to him. "When will you be back?"

"I'm not sure." Eva had implied she was returning. Thank god. Maybe this task wouldn't be as bad as he feared. "A few days, maybe longer."

Felix frowned but didn't ask any questions. "Contact Ma, will you? She's been worried about— *What the fuck*?"

Saber whirled and saw the shuttle they'd borrowed shimmer out of sight. He strode to where they'd parked it, walking straight through the empty air. "Fuck, that's all kinds of disturbing." An understatement.

"It's lucky we flew straight here," Eva said, her cheeks bleached of color. "What if it had disappeared while we were in flight? We could have died."

Saber went to her and pulled her against his chest. "We made it here in one piece, kitten." He stared over her head, his gaze connecting with Felix's before he closed his eyes. He could have lost her, and that didn't bear thinking about.

Eva pulled away to glance down at her clothes, her expression one of horror. "Do you think our clothes will vanish?"

"Could be quite a show," Felix said, a lazy grin taking root on his features as his gaze did a visual sweep of Eva.

Saber's feral snarl charged from his throat without warning, and Felix straightened, his expression wiping clean. "Your call," he said to Eva once Felix backed away two steps. "We'll lose time because my mother will want to meet you and feed us."

She swallowed visibly. "Let's risk it. Can't be worse than a cooking pot."

It felt strange being back on Dalcon. They left the shuttle at the spaceport and walked the short distance to the market, Eva leading Saber through the dark alleyways with confidence. The city was crowded and seemed much noisier than she recalled. People—strangers—pressed close, and the smells made her nose wrinkle in distaste. She felt out of step even though she was confident no one would eat them here or openly attack them unless they were on the Dearbhorgaill payroll.

Saber stayed close, a solid presence at her back as she skirted a smelly pile of garbage in the middle of the alley. Eva held her breath to avoid inhaling the stench and gave thanks she wasn't barefoot. Not yet, at any rate.

"How much farther?" Saber asked.

"At the end of the alley and to the right. This alley opens onto a wide lane, the main thoroughfare of the market."

"Hey, Eva," a voice called from behind a fruit stall. "Where you been, lady?"

"On holiday, Jimbo," she said. "How is Maria?"

"Good, good. There bin trouble at your rest'rant," he said.

Eva's stomach plummeted at his words, even though she'd expected the Dearbhorgaills would wreak havoc during her absence. "I'm back now."

"Who he?"

"Saber Mitchell," Saber said, moving forward to stand at Eva's side.

"Who-ee. He a big 'un." Jimbo gave a laugh that bore a faint air of nerves.

"Talk to you later," Eva said and lengthened her strides. Saber kept pace, walking at her side in silence. He was watchful though, his gaze never still as he kept tabs on their surroundings and the people of the market.

Several waved at her and let out cheerful calls of greeting, but no one approached her and Saber.

"This is one of my restaurants," she said, her heart sinking upon seeing the boarded-up windows. At least it was open. She started for the door, but Saber stopped her.

"I'll go first."

Eva gave a swift nod, following him inside.

"A table for two?" a familiar voice asked.

"Robbie," Eva said. "Where is the solar light?" The few candles weren't providing much illumination, apart from showing her they had no customers.

"Eva! You're back! Thank the lady." He rushed to embrace her, his cane tapping the stone floor but came to an abrupt halt at Saber's warning snarl.

"Saber, stop that!" Eva said. "This is Robbie Campbell, my assistant and co-conspirator. And *friend*," she said firmly. "This is Saber Mitchell."

Saber growled again, but this time, the sound wasn't as pronounced. Eva scowled and decided to ignore him. "What's going on?" she asked.

"Lady Almeda Dearbhorgaill came in person, with a bully-boy, to retrieve the currency transfer certificates. She was very put out when you weren't here, and we couldn't contact you. She was desperate for your signature."

"On what?"

"She didn't say."

"Why don't we have any customers?"

"The stock deliveries have dried up, our solar-light contact was vandalized, and the new one hasn't come yet. Everything that could go wrong *has* gone wrong," Robbie said simply. "I've tried, Eva. I tried to keep everything going. The other restaurant has fared about the same. We're lucky if we have a dozen customers each day."

"I see," said Eva. "And the balance of our account with the bank?"

"Lady Almeda has taken everything. Just as we planned."

"Good. You close up here. I want to start taking notes and do a quick stocktake." Eva paused to study her friend with concern. "Robbie, you need to take care. I don't want you getting hurt in the backlash."

Robbie nodded. "What about the other restaurant?"

"I'll stop by and tell them to close. I'm surprised I have staff left."

Robbie winced. "Not many."

"And the building on the third restaurant?"

Robbie winced yet again. "It's come to a halt."

A pained sound escaped, and desolation kicked her in the guts. Bloody *dromgoose* Dearbhorgaills.

Saber slipped a comforting arm around her waist. "We can fix this."

Eva bit back her pain. When Pryce was alive, his parents hadn't been quite as dedicated in destroying everything he'd built. And now she was failing her husband.

"Kitten, it's time to play hardball. They're bullies, and you need to stand up to them."

"He's right," Robbie said. "They murdered their son, and they should pay."

"Why are you so sure they're responsible for their son's death?" Saber asked.

"The marketplace is full of gossip," Eva said. "There were rumors."

"Have you followed the rumors to the source?"

"No. Robbie and I have spent every waking moment trying to keep the restaurants afloat."

Saber nodded. "Take care of your plan, sort out the problems. Submit a formal complaint."

"Most of the lawmen are in their pockets," Robbie said.

"There must be someone," Saber said. "How are you intending to spring your trap?"

"I intend to dress in my finest gown and petition the King of Dalcon for an audience. I met him once when Pryce took me to a court ball. He struck me as a fair man."

"Do it but take Robbie with you to witness their skullduggery. Gather names from others in the market who have witnessed the

Dearbhorgaills' tactics. Embarrass and shame them in front of their peers, but do a good job of it because a wounded enemy is a dangerous one. You don't want to give them a chance to regroup."

Eva nodded, seeing the sense of his words. She needed a perfect plan in place before she pushed the Dearbhorgaills. "What are *you* going to do?"

Saber brushed her cheek with his fingertips. "I'm going to investigate your husband's death and discover who killed him. Add another layer of damming proof against your in-laws. Where is your place?"

Eva rattled off the address, befuddled.

"I'll meet you there later tonight. Keep safe." He pulled her in for a hard kiss then set her away and strode from the empty restaurant.

"Where did you meet him?" Robbie asked, staring after Saber. "I like a man of action."

So did she. "At the resort. He owns it." She sucked in a deep breath and righted her rioting senses. "Let's do this stocktake, and then I'll deliver the second payment to the lawyer."

They worked together for most of the afternoon. Eva took great satisfaction in delivering the mortgage payment with money she'd hidden away, and returned to the restaurant before darkness fell to retrieve Robbie. "Let's go to the other restaurant. We'll document everything that's gone wrong there and find proof where we can. I'll send a com to the palace and beg an audience at the next people sessions. When are the next sessions? Do you know?"

"In three solar days, I think. Sometimes, they have two a week if there is a demand."

"*Frying fungus.* We'll be lucky if we get on the list."

"It's worth a try. My cousin works the people sessions. I'll consult with him," Robbie said.

Eva locked the door and set a rapid pace to get to her second restaurant, which was in a better part of town. Even so, she jumped at the slightest noise, her gaze darting left and right, assessing every hint of danger. Robbie limped beside her and rattled off facts and figures, oblivious to her tension. She tried to listen, she really did. Difficult to concentrate when she was forced to walk through the marketplace after dark.

Especially after the attack not long before her trip to Tiraq…

Relief struck her when the sign for her restaurant came into sight.

"Right," she said, pushing open the door. "Go to the office. We need a list of the damages here. Add the names of witnesses—as many as you can—while I speak with Junita."

"Yes, boss."

Eva glanced around the restaurant—the sparse furniture, the lack of customers, the badly cracked mirror behind the bar, and the lack of drinking stock.

The buxom restaurant manager sported a black eye, and her bright-blue hair tendrils waved in unceasing motion—a sure sign of her agitation. Her bodice was laced tight, her black dress and white apron pristine, but she walked with a pronounced limp and leaned heavily on a crutch.

"What happened, Junita?"

"I tried to stop Lady Almeda and her sidekick from taking the contents of the safe," Junita said in a stiff voice.

Despondency ripped through Eva's carefully built defenses. No matter what she did, no matter how hard she tried, the Dearbhorgaills seemed to win. She was so tired. Tired of fighting, battling, struggling to keep Pryce's dream alive. All she wanted to do was cook and plan menus, present good food that people talked about for solar days after they'd eaten in one of her restaurants. Her eyes started to sting, but she clenched her hands to fists, the pain of her nails digging into her palms giving her focus.

She would not break.

She'd go through with this plan.

It would work. It had too.

"Okay, Junita. Robbie is in the office. Give him the details of what happened and when. He'll record the information." Junita sashayed away, her blue tendrils calmer now, and Eva sighed as she scanned the empty restaurant.

Saber was right. Documenting everything to present at once built a better case, and would support the most damning proof—the currency transfer certificates she'd inscribed with special ink, a concoction of her own devise made from the juice of a limonadoc fruit. She had the certificate numbers, and once they were matched with where they were spent and she made the ink react, it would become clear they were stolen.

Hmm, maybe some of the market dwellers had even seen Lady Almeda in the market.

Strange that she'd risked a visit.

Eva's brow furrowed. Maybe she should do a little sleuthing of her own.

Saber strolled the market from stall to stall, asking questions and pumping the stallholders for information. Even though he was a stranger, it was remarkably easy to gain information. The Dearbhorgaills had attacked one of their own. Everyone loved Eva.

He approached a red mumber after a stallholder had directed him to the tavern where the male worked and asked his questions.

The swarthy red man eyed him up and down. "What's it to you?"

"Eva Henry is my woman, and I don't take kindly to folks upsetting her." Saber wasn't intimidated by the man's height or his fists, which were almost the size of dinner plates.

The red mumber shifted his gaze first, his red skin taking on a deeper hue—caused, Saber knew, by strong emotions. "Used to work for the Dearbhorgaills as security in their home. Lady Almeda took exception to my color. Said I clashed with the uniform and the furnishings."

No question of loyalty here. "Do you know who ordered the hit on Pryce Dearbhorgaill? Who carried it out?"

"Yes."

"Who?"

"Depends what you do with the information," the red mumber said. "If you intend to take legal action against the shooter or punish him in another manner, I refuse to tell you."

"I'll pay for the information." Somehow he'd squeeze the money out of his budget to help Eva. Her current situation wouldn't be so bad if he hadn't kidnapped her and kept her from returning to Dalcon.

"Goes without sayin'," the red mumber said. "But if you intend to hunt down the killer or bring him to trial for murdering a toff, I ain't playin'. The man has suffered enough. The lord 'n' lady forced him to do it, threatened if he didn't kill the man, his wife and his kids would die." The red mumber curled his top lip to bare big square teeth, the front one of which was missing. "What would you do for the ones you love?"

"I'd kill," Saber said.

The red mumber nodded as if he'd made his point.

"The Dearbhorgaills are trying to hurt the woman I love," Saber said, deciding to play it straight from the gut. "They're trying to destroy her when all she wants is to live in peace and run her restaurants. I'm collecting information," Saber said. "Because I intend to bring them down."

"Would a signed statement help?"

"Yes. How did they pay him?"

The red mumber's lip curled again. "They released his wife and son from captivity once the deed was done."

"Where were his family held? Could I get a signed statement from people there?"

"I'll give you one. Pretty sure the other men would cooperate, long as they don't get dragged out and punished," the red mumber said.

"You have my word," Saber said. "All I'm interested in doing is taking down the Dearbhorgaills."

"The lady be the worst. The lord stays at his club, doesn't go home much these days from what I hear."

Saber bought the man a drink and arranged to return with gratitude payments in exchange for the sworn statements.

All in all, a good few hours' work. Saber strolled through the streets, keeping a close watch for cutpurses. God, he missed Tiraq and the resort. The clean air of the island. The sooner he talked Eva into leaving this shithole, the better.

He arrived at Penny Lane and knocked on the door of number eight. The door opened seconds after his knock, and Eva stood before him.

"I have a hearing with the king," she said. "Robbie's cousin came through for us."

"The bribe of a ginger cake swung it," Robbie called from somewhere behind her.

"I'll make him two," Eva said.

Saber stepped inside and closed the door, shutting out the street's hustle. "When is your hearing?"

"Tomorrow," Eva said. "Earlier than we thought. I have some of the documentation ready and can gather the rest in the morning."

"I've discovered who murdered your husband," Saber said and cursed his bluntness when the color fled her cheeks. He reached out and drew her against him, angry at himself for causing her distress.

"Go ahead," she said. "No, wait. Come into the other room. I'll make us something to eat while we talk."

"Do you need me?" Robbie asked.

"Tomorrow morning. Early," she added. "We have a lot of work to do before our audience."

"Right you are," Robbie said, and limped to the door.

"Robbie." Eva stayed him with a hand on his arm. "Be careful walking home. I'd never forgive myself if something happened to you."

"See you tomorrow," Robbie said.

Once he'd left, Saber locked the door.

"This way," Eva said, leading the way into a room off the entrance. It was full of solar light, with stone counters, a sparkling hot cube, and a cool cube. "I stopped at my favorite market stall to purchase supplies."

"How bad are things with the restaurants?"

"Nuisance stuff. The customers will return once the trouble is settled."

Saber stalked the length of the room, needing to burn off excess energy. "I talked to a red mumber. He knows the killer but says he was blackmailed into committing the offense. Said the Dearbhorgaills had his wife and son stashed away and threatened to kill them if he didn't do as instructed."

"Doesn't surprise me. Will he come forward?"

Saber fingered the leaf of a bright-copper plant. "He's frightened of the repercussions."

"Again, that doesn't surprise me."

"He's willing to give a signed statement, plus some of the staff who worked where the wife and son were jailed will give you statements."

"I can pay them," Eva said. "I wasn't stupid enough to leave all my currency in my account. You should have seen the surprised and dismayed expression on the lawyer's face when I arrived with the second payment this afternoon. He knows what they're doing."

"Clever girl."

"You know, I'm so tired of this crap. After this is over, I'm going to consider relocating. A place Bluebird will enjoy."

Saber sucked in a rapid breath. "I thought Bluebird would stay at the resort."

"Not likely," Eva said, and he wished he could see her face, but she'd turned away to stir something in a pot.

"Do you think the king will listen?" Saber asked, changing the subject before he snapped out something he shouldn't in sheer frustration. He'd chased her once, and he'd do it again without hesitation.

"From what I know and have seen, he seems a fair man. I'll do my best to get justice for Pryce."

Eva served a meaty sauce on top of noodles. It looked and tasted a lot like spaghetti Bolognese. They ate quietly until Saber eased back his chair, relaxed with a full belly.

"Tell me about the black cat here on my shoulder."

He sat upright. "I'm tired," he said. "Let's go to bed."

"I have a spare room."

Saber stood and rounded the table to stand by her chair. "I sleep where you sleep."

"I thought that was just while we were together on Tiraq?"

"No."

Eva stared at his set face, felt a tiny jolt go through her body. She stood, as he so obviously wanted, and led the way up the stairs to her bedroom.

"Did Pryce live with you here?" His tone was clipped now.

"Yes."

"This was your bedroom?" Still abrupt.

"It was, but I've changed it since he died. It reminded me too much of him."

"Good." Saber's fingers went to his green shirt, and he

unfastened the tabs to display his hard chest. "I'm trying to be reasonable, but jealousy keeps raising its annoying head."

"I..." She paused, wondering if she should tell him the truth. Then began again with a sigh. "I didn't love Pryce. I tried." She squeezed her eyes shut. "I really tried."

"Shush." He wrapped his arms around her and held her against his chest. He was always holding her, touching her. "You were happy with him, and I'm sure he was happy too."

"He was always smiling," she said.

"What did I tell you? Happy."

"I hope so." *Frying fungus*, she hoped she'd made Pryce content, hoped he hadn't felt the lack, that he had in fact mistaken her gratitude for fonder feelings. They'd slept together, worked together, and she'd found happiness in almost all areas of their marriage.

"Clothes off," he said with his usual bossiness.

A laugh spilled out. "You just want to see me naked."

"Correct." He stepped back, cocked one hip against the wall, and folded his hands across his broad chest. A tiny grin played on his lips. "I'd appreciate that very much."

Eva bent to remove her boots, but before she could put fingers to fastenings, her clothes started dissolving. She gaped at her legs and watched her trews, the rest of her clothes fade from sight until she stood in front of Saber, naked.

"How convenient," Saber said and prowled toward her, smirk lighting his sexy green eyes.

Eva opened her mouth, snapped it shut, and opened it again. "Why haven't *your* clothes disappeared?"

His smirk widened, his gaze doing a thorough survey of her nakedness. "Because I wished harder."

Eva tried covering herself.

"Are you turning shy?" Saber's hands settled on her shoulders, his amusement in full bloom. It made her more self-conscious.

"You're beautiful." His breath caressed her face as he moved her toward the bed. She toppled backward, legs splayed, and he stepped into the space between them.

"Your clothes are still on." She wouldn't mind a better visual.

"I can fix that," he said in a silky voice. He took off his shirt and tossed it aside. His boots clomped onto the floor, and he peeled his trews down his legs. "Now can we move to the next stage?"

"Your clothes didn't disappear."

"Nope." He ran his hand over her thigh, making her breath catch in anticipation. "I have a theory."

"Do tell." She suppressed a shiver with difficulty and judging by the flash of white teeth; he knew what his touch was doing to her.

"When we were at the ruins, things appeared after we thought about them. Once they were no longer needed, they disappeared." His fingers teased the delicate skin behind her knee.

She bit her lip. "L-Like the shuttle."

"Right," he said. "I presume you have other clothes here at your dwelling."

"I do."

"I don't have any spare clothes, which is why I think these have remained solid and real. Once we return to the resort or I purchase new clothes, these will disappear."

He wanted her to return to the resort with him? She *had* mentioned relocating...but what about the restaurants?

They don't mean anything without Pryce.

The thought flashed through her mind, along with the truth of it. The restaurants were more his dream. When she considered her life after the Dearbhorgaills, the goal wasn't managing three restaurants on her own forever. There had to be more than hard work and worry. But what? That was the question.

Saber's fingers slipped lower on her thigh and drifted closer to her pussy. Everything in her froze, waiting, praying for contact.

"Y-you'll have to let me know if your theory is correct." He made her stutter. A sad state of affairs.

"You'll come home with me," Saber said, brooking no refusal.

"But the restaurants—"

"You belong with *me*."

Her mouth opened and closed in an imitation of the lippy-fish sold in the market. The entire time she stared at his hard face, trying to understand exactly what he wanted.

He loomed over her, pressing her into the sleep-bed with his bulk. He didn't stop until his face was inches from hers. "You are *mine*, and I'm not leaving you here alone. I have to return to the resort and my family, but I need something for myself, someone solely for me. I need *you*, Eva."

"Me? But I'm nobody—"

"Bullshit. You're special. You might have been discarded as a child, but the people in the market kept you safe. Everyone I spoke with knew you, admired you. They spoke well of you. Pryce married you because he held you in high regard, and if he were alive, you'd still be with him and happy. I get that. But I want a slice of happiness too. I want you, Eva. Come home with me. Make the resort your home. Sell your restaurants here or keep them. I don't care. You can have free rein to run the restaurant at the resort, or you can open one in the village if that's what you want." He stared at her intently, his eyes flickering to cat and back. "I don't care what you do as long as you spend every night in my bed with me."

Eva gaped at him, shocked by the passion in his voice, the determination to get what he wanted.

Her.

When she remained silent, he groaned, the sound holding a trace of self-derision. "Not going to say anything?" he asked in that silky voice of his, the one he used when his emotions came to the fore. "Maybe I'll demonstrate what I mean."

And with that, he pounced.

Chapter Twelve

H is mouth went straight to her neck and the minute tattoo there. Eve wondered at its origin. Maybe it had something to do with the weird ghost house and the gentleman? Then that thought—*every* thought in her head—faded as his tongue rasped across the tattoo.

Her body jerked at the arc of pleasure radiating through her body. His hands were everywhere, skimming her breasts, tugging at a nipple, smoothing over her hip. And his mouth teased the tattoo, sucking, licking, driving her crazy.

She heard a sound, a hungry little noise, and realized it came from her. A heated flush moved down her body, and the tattoo pulsed, coming alive under his ministrations.

Moisture formed between her legs, a ferocious flood. He lifted his head, his eyes of freaky cat green that should have scared her but didn't. He was hard and determined—a delectable combination—and she had no defenses against him, realized she didn't *want* any.

He plundered her mouth with a kiss designed to inflame and consume. Whimpers fell from her mouth, demands she couldn't contain.

She gasped for air, parted their lips enough to get out her desperate words. "Saber. Fuck me. Please."

He growled—a mean, bad-tempered growl—as if she'd said the wrong thing, but his touch didn't change. Instead he parted her legs and rose over her, his face harsh, eyes glittering.

Then he positioned himself and plunged inside her with one hard stroke.

Eva screamed as fire exploded inside her. Every particle of her body pulled tight then snapped under so much pleasure it hurt. She convulsed around his cock, shuddering and bucking as he thrust inside her again and again.

Eva pulled his head down for a kiss and inhaled his raw male desire. His muscles rippled, and primitive hunger etched into his face as their lips met.

She held his sweaty body as he continued to hammer into her, a primal sense of satisfaction rolling through her. Saber gave a strangled moan and came. Came with a bellow of sound that echoed in her bedroom.

Gradually, he relaxed and twisted their bodies so he wasn't a heavy weight on her chest. Neither said anything, but Eva's stomach went all fluttery. Her gaze went to his strong jawline, his sensual lips, then wandered up to his eyes and came to an abrupt halt.

He was watching her, gaze impassive, yet somehow she sensed his uncertainty, his turmoil—the same riot of emotions churning through her mind now that she could think again.

"We belong together," he said. "Once your problems are sorted, we're going home to the resort. Decide what you want to do with your restaurants."

A definite order, and Eva couldn't find the energy to dispute his high-handedness. *Not when that's what you want,* her conscience whispered. She ran her fingers across his chest and played with one of his nipples. "Why is the resort so important to you?"

"My *family* is important to me," he corrected, his voice back to its normal gravelly rumble. "Family is important to all felines. On Earth, cats are solitary creatures but not feline shifters. We do better with family and friends around us. Our ancestors proved that. They built a community with strong ties, and until the virus came, we were solid."

"Do you argue?" Eva had never known the family he described and couldn't imagine herself as part of it. She didn't enjoy the idea of being an outsider.

But wasn't it a bit like that in the market? There was part of the market, the people who had taken her in, who stuck together and looked out for each other.

"Of course. We all have strong personalities."

"But the resort is important. You don't want to fail."

"If the resort fails, we'll have nothing," Saber said simply

"Did you do something similar on Earth?" She moved on to playing with his hair, enjoying tugging the long strands.

"We were farmers. I thought I'd mentioned that? And we had the vineyards, of course." His hand ran up and down her back and she whispered out a breath of relief. He'd lost the air of tension and seemed more himself.

"Then why a resort?"

"I won it in a card game. I staked the last of our money, and when the game was over, my family owned a run-down resort."

"That was...um...risky."

"Not really," he said, something almost self-deprecating in his smile. He caught her gaze and held it. "I had no intention of losing. I cheated."

Eva blinked, realized he was laying himself bare, and wasn't sure how to react.

"Sorry you slept with me now?"

Saber regretted cheating. She saw it in him but also that he'd do it again if the need arose. His family came first—and he wanted to include *her* in that family. She sucked in a quick breath, gave a disbelieving shake of her head. *Frying fungus.*

"You make me feel good. Why would I be sorry?" No. She was uncertain, she thought. Frightened to take a step into the unknown when she was comfortable here on Dalcon. She'd known upfront of Pryce's parents' hatred, their dislike of her humble roots. They'd wanted Pryce to remain in his designated caste, not to marry a guttersnipe who didn't even belong to a caste.

Saber's family didn't know her. She'd seen them at the resort, probably unknowingly spoken to some of them. What if it turned out they hated her? If she left Dalcon, sold her restaurants...

Gods, she need to think about this. Hard.

Saber wanted to spring off the bed and curse. He wanted to shake Eva, tell her they were meant for each other. Of course, he could just tell her he suspected they were mates and they wouldn't do well—either of them—if they tried to live on different planets. Yeah, he could do that. But he *needed* her to want him.

To come to the decision on her own to be with him.

He wanted to know she valued him, cared for him.

He craved her love.

And damn, didn't that make him a stupid sap?

Instead of having a tantrum to dispel his frustration, he nuzzled her neck, breathed in her scent, and began making love to her again.

And it *was* making love rather than sex. They mightn't have known each other long, but he knew the difference between lust and love. They'd seen each other at their best and worst, and strong bonds came with adversity.

He snorted inwardly. The sort that echoed the mate bond.

He gripped the taut globes of her ass and pulled her closer, letting her feel his lengthening shaft, his need for her. She hesitated but kissed him back, twirled her tongue with his.

At least this was one area where they were in perfect accord.

He kissed her deeply, letting her have it rough and raw. Imprinting himself on her, body and mind. Then he eased the kiss, turning it lazy with the stroke of his tongue. She gave a purring sound of approval, and he smiled against her lips.

"More," she said when he nibbled her bottom lip.

"Not a problem." He nuzzled her neck, bypassing the tattoo and heading for her breasts. The nipples puckered the instant he gave them a long lick. So responsive. His hands wandered lower, slipped between her legs. She twisted against his body, struggled to give him plenty of room.

His nostrils flared at the scent of arousal filling the air. Mouthwatering, it steeped him in lust.

"Come inside me," she said.

"I want to take you from behind."

"Any way you want," she whispered, her body pliant as he rearranged her on the sleep-bed. He moved over her, sank his cock into her damp heat and a primal sense of satisfaction filled him. He kissed the space between her shoulder blades then moved his mouth across to the tattoo. Unable to resist, he licked her silky flesh and his pulse picked up in speed. She groaned, the lustful sound pushing him to drive into her faster.

Once again, he climaxed hard, unable to hold back the pleasure backing up inside him like a mountain avalanche. He had enough presence of mind to strum his fingers across her clit, make it good for her while he still had a few brain cells functioning.

"That's it. Come for me."

She moaned, the throaty sound twisting another spasm from his cock. "Saber."

"Enjoy my name on your lips, kitten."

"*Saber!*"

"Let go. I want to hear you cry out in pleasure. Let me feel it, Eva. Show me how good my cock makes you feel." He gave a feral grin and rubbed again.

When she started quaking, he gave her more until the tension snapped in her straining body.

"Perfect," he said, his voice emerging in a ragged whisper. "You're fuckin' perfect."

She wriggled from his grasp when her breathing eased and turned to look up at him. "I'm hungry."

"Yeah?"

"Yeah. Want something to eat?"

Saber climbed off the sleep-bed. "I'll get you something."

"I have legs."

Saber brushed a lock of hair from her face. "Don't you get it, kitten? I derive pleasure from doing things for you." His gaze settled on her breasts. "*With* you."

"I'm used to looking after myself."

"I know, but I'm willing to shoulder some of the burden. Remember that, kitten, and think about it."

Eva thought about Saber's words the next morning when she left to meet Robbie. She thought about them throughout the morning and continued to do so when she returned to her lodgings to dress for her audience with the king.

She clomped down the passage to the reception room of her lodgings. Robbie was seated at Pryce's old desk, going through the accounts for the restaurants.

"Any word from Saber?" she asked.

"Not yet. What are you going to do if he doesn't come?"

"He'll get the info we need," she said. "And if he doesn't, we'll go with what we have. It's pretty damning on its own."

"Not many people cross swords with the Dearbhorgaills," Robbie said. "Your life won't be worth living if the king rejects your claims."

Eva's mouth hardened. Pryce had died. Others had been hurt, often when Lady Almeda didn't get her way. It wasn't right for the ruling classes to hold so much power over the lower-caste inhabitants on Dalcon. "I'll face that if it happens. At the very least, Lady Almeda will feel the embarrassment of hearing her name on the lips of gossips. She won't enjoy the rumors at her expense."

Robbie checked his timepiece. "We have to leave for the palace. We can't wait any longer."

"Very well," Eva said.

The fly-mo journey to the palace didn't take long, but Eva felt as if she were entering another world when security let their driver through the main gates leading into the palace.

Robbie gave the guards on the inner wall their names, and Eva waited anxiously while they consulted their list. There was always an outside chance that one of the Dearbhorgaills had been told about her upcoming audience.

The fly-mo driver came to a halt at a third security gate. "This is as far as I can go. Do you wish me to wait for you?"

"Yes, please," Eva said, handing over several currency notes.

Guards checked her bag for weapons and patted down Robbie. Once the guards were satisfied, they were allowed to enter the main palace grounds.

Gardens full of colorful flowers of every hue imaginable caught her eye. In the distance, a large oval-shaped pond glinted in the solar sun. White gravel paths wound between the gardens and knee-high hedges, and several pagodas with elegant spires and decorations offered places to rest and while away the solar day.

"Come along," a man said in a testy tone. "The king is a busy man."

Eva turned to glimpse a rotund man wearing a deep-purple robe over his shoulders. A matching turban wound around his head, highlighting his round face. A crease between his eyes indicated his mood. Impatient.

"I'm sorry," she said.

"Come along," the man repeated, snapping his fingers in her direction. He trotted off, obviously expecting them to hurry.

Robbie gave a wry shrug and limped after him. Eva sighed. She hadn't been nervous, but now that she and Robbie followed the courtier, nerves swirled through her stomach, recoiling and rebounding like a mindless, panicked creature attempting to escape a predator.

She trotted after the man, keeping her gaze on the swirl of his purple cloak as he navigated a maze of corridors within the palace. They reached a room full of courtiers and citizens of Dalcon. The famed audience room.

"Wait here," the man said.

"*Flaming fungus*," Robbie said in an urgent whisper. "The king is never going to get through this many people. I'm sorry, Eva. I've wasted your time."

"We'll wait," Eva said in a firm voice. "Let's find a seat. They seem to be moving in and out quickly enough."

Eva kept an eye on the door. Every few minutes, a courtier in white came out, consulted a list, and hollered a name.

"Look who's here," Robbie said, tugging her arm.

"Who?" Eva's gaze followed the direction Robbie indicated, and her stomach swooped into freefall. She squeezed against the wall and attempted to look inconspicuous.

Lady Almeda and Lord Loeiz Dearbhorgaill, dressed in their finest clothing and pressing the flesh.

Robbie leaned closer. "Do you think their presence is a coincidence?"

"I don't know." Eva studied their easy posture and how they circulated, chatting with other men and women waiting for their turn to speak with the king.

The first thing she and Robbie had done when they'd entered the room was to scrutinize everyone anticipating an audience. Neither of the Dearbhorgaills had done the same. Because they'd *known* she was here, had seen the contents of the request she'd completed. Or someone had told them.

Either way, it didn't bode well for her petition.

"I wish Saber had turned up with the proof he said he'd get," Robbie said. "It would make all the difference."

"I know."

"The evidence we have now mightn't be enough," Robbie continued.

"I know," Eva repeated. "We'll go with what we have and make the best of it."

The courtier in white came out and called the next name.

"How much longer, you think?" Robbie asked.

"I couldn't say. You said we were at the end of the list."

Robbie sighed loudly. "Yes."

"Then we wait and hope for the best." Eva studied her hands and concentrated on her breathing. She could do this. She imagined Pryce standing at her shoulder and urging her to do her best. In her mind, she heard Pryce encouraging her to face his parents and stand tall.

That was all anyone could ask of her.

"Eva Henry," the courtier intoned.

Robbie stood. "I'm coming too. I'm not letting you face them alone."

"Thanks." Just knowing Robbie intended to stand with her lent steel to her spine. She strode toward the waiting courtier, garbed in a scarlet gown Pryce had purchased for her to wear to a court function. Chin up in a determined jut, Robbie limped at her side.

"Only you," the courtier said.

"No. I need my assistant to accompany me since he has pertinent information to my petition."

The courtier looked Robbie up and down, took in the well-worn but clean black trews and shirt, his cane. He sniffed but nodded grudgingly. "This way."

The king's audience room made Eva's steps falter. Gold glinted off every surface and blue stones—the color of royalty—ran around the wall in a decorative trim. Pryce had visited the king here. They were of a similar age and had known each other well. They'd been friends, which still caused wonder to well in Eva.

Her gaze hit the king where he sat on his ornate throne, and it flitted away when she recalled that Pryce used to joke and say he'd seen the king naked. He was a royal, all right. No doubts there, since his equipment was apparently also blue, as rumor held.

Heat flooded her cheeks, and a sharp nudge from Robbie's elbow jerked her back. *Frying fungus*, she thought as she sank into a deep curtsy. *Mind out of the drain.*

"Your m-majesty," she managed. After long seconds, she rose, her tongue flicking out to dampen her lips. What now? How to start? Did she plunge right into her grievance or wait for the king to signal she should start?

Before she could decide, the courtier dressed in white started to read from his genic mini-tab. "Eva Henry, widow of Lord Pryce Dearbhorgaill," he intoned. "She is here to air her grievance regarding Lord Loeiz and Lady Almeda Dearbhorgaill. I have taken the liberty of summoning the Lord and Lady so they might rebut her words."

The king sent her a piercing look, a warning he was no mere figurehead in this principality. His eyes were a vivid violet and so pretty she wanted to stare. She didn't. Instead she took a deep breath and waited.

"Bring Lord and Lady Dearbhorgaill into my chamber. We will hear the charges together to expedite the matter."

"Yes, Your Majesty." The courtier marched to the door and opened it.

Eva heard him ask the Dearbhorgaills to enter. Before he could shut the door, muffled screams and curses rose. Male shouts. Women's screams.

The king rose, hand planted firmly on a laser weapon strapped to his side. "What is it, Turlow?"

Before the courtier could reply, a large black cat charged into the room. A satchel was tied around his neck, and it bounced as Saber ran.

In her peripheral vision, Eva saw the king take aim. "Don't shoot!" She jumped in front of the laser weapon. "Please. He's with me."

Saber halted by her side and licked her hand before sitting on his haunches.

"A-are you s-sure?" Robbie whispered, backing away. "He's awful big."

"He's fine," Eva said and petted Saber on his head, scratching behind his head. She ignored Saber's sharp snarl of protest and continued to run her hand over his soft fur.

The king hesitated, but when Saber pressed against her and purred, he thrust his laser weapon away and sat on his throne.

Lord and Lady Dearbhorgaill entered the audience chamber at a dignified stroll. They came to a halt, their faces bearing identical appalled expressions.

"Your Majesty," Lord Dearbhorgaill said. "Is that creature safe?"

"I am assuming the animal is harmless," the king said. "Ms. Henry seems to have it under her control."

Eva wasn't so sure about that. With each stroke of her hand, she felt the tension in Saber's muscular body. Robbie wasn't accepting her assurances either, because he moved to her other side, his stance as stiff as a fire poker.

"Ms. Henry," the king said. "Please give me a précis of your grievances."

"Lord and Lady Dearbhorgaill have made my life a living hell, Your Majesty. They have gone out of their way to create difficulties for me and my restaurants."

"Preposterous," Lord Loeiz snapped.

The king held up a hand, and Lord Dearbhorgaill's face took on a pained expression.

"While I was away recently, Lady Dearbhorgaill barged into one of my restaurants and stole three blank currency forms. I also have reason to believe they arranged a contract on Lord Pryce, and as a result, my husband was murdered in the market. Lastly, they have called in favors from their contemporaries to ensure I was unable to borrow to finance my third restaurant. Only one company offered me finance, and I have since discovered the Dearbhorgaills are behind the offer. They make it difficult for me to meet my loan repayments by ordering their underlings to vandalize my existing restaurants. They create disturbances to drive away my customers and spread rumors of food poisoning. You name the means, and they've used them to damage my businesses and my reputation."

"I see." The king glanced at the Dearbhorgaills, then back at her, and stroked his chin. "Do you have proof of your accusations?"

"Your majesty!" Lord Dearbhorgaill sent her a murderous glare. "Surely you don't believe the word of this...this common trollop?"

"She's a guttersnipe!" Lady Almeda snapped. "Brought up in the market. She has no morals. She's a thief and a liar."

Saber snarled, and Eva pressed a firm hand on his furry shoulders. "Stay," she whispered.

"Quiet," the king said to the Dearbhorgaills in a firm voice. "What proof do you have, Ms. Henry?"

"I have documentation in my bag, Your Majesty. They prove

Lady Dearbhorgaill stole currency certificates from me. I also have statements from people who live in the market. They witnessed the vandalizing of my restaurants plus some of the other bully tactics employed by the Dearbhorgaill underlings."

The king held out his hand. "I'll see them."

Lady Almeda sent her a vicious glare. "But—"

"Quiet," the king barked.

Eva retrieved the documents she and Robbie had collected during the previous day. "These are sworn statements of witness accounts, plus I have retrieved the canceled currency certificates from my banker. I should explain that before my recent absence, I wrote with special ink on the currency certificates, and my banker and two employees witnessed this." She handed the certificates to the king.

He peered at the certificates. "I see nothing out of the ordinary about the certificates."

"May I, Your Majesty?" Eva stepped closer. "Firstly, each certificate is numbered. You will see that the numbers match the numbers recorded in the witnessed document here. The ink requires heat in order to be read. I have a steam apparatus in my bag. It will produce enough heat to react with the invisible ink."

"Intriguing. Turlow, I shall require you to witness this process," the king said.

"Your majesty," Lord Loeiz protested. "Are you truly going to believe the word of this trollop?"

Eva noted Lady Almeda's cheeks were scarlet with fury, her hands curled like claws at her sides. "Everyone knows she's a liar! She tricked our son into marriage, and now she seeks to destroy our lives!"

"Quiet!" the king thundered. "Or I'll have you forcibly removed from the audience room."

Lady Almeda's mouth snapped shut, and she glowered in Eva's direction. And perhaps looked a little worried.

"Show me the ink," the king ordered.

Eva pulled the steamer from her bag. Robbie held the certificate as she waved the heat across the portion where she'd written in the special ink. Slowly, words formed on the paper.

"Amazing." The king exchanged a glance with the courtier.

"What does it say?" Lord Loeiz demanded.

"Whatever it says is a lie," Lady Almeda snapped.

"Read the words for Lord and Lady Dearbhorgaill," the king said to his courtier.

The man retrieved a pair of eyeglasses from an inner pocket, accepted the certificate from Robbie and started to read. "This certificate is the property of Eva Henry. It is to be used for petty cash, and the amount of this certificate must not exceed twenty-five shillars."

"And how much is the certificate made out for, Turlow?" the king asked.

"Ten thousand shillars, your majesty."

"Check the ink on the other two certificates, Turlow," the king said.

A weighty silence pulsed in the audience room while the courtier activated the ink with Robbie's help.

"They are the same, Your Majesty," the courtier said. "Except they are made out for higher amounts. Twenty-five thousand shillars and fifty thousand shillars."

The king focused his glare on the Dearbhorgaills. "What do you have to say about this?"

"We have no knowledge of these certificates," Lord Loeiz said. "This is a travesty!"

"They didn't sign the certificates," the king said. "I presume that is your signature?"

"Yes, Your Majesty. But when I left Dalcon, the certificates were locked in a safe. They are also dated when I was away, and the writing on the certificates—apart from my signature—belongs to neither me nor my assistant. I believe you'll find it is Lady Almeda's writing."

"It's a forgery!" Lady Almeda snarled and took two steps toward Eva, her expression murderous.

Saber snarled and shifted position to place himself between the two women. Lady Almeda froze in place.

Eva continued, "I believe you'd also find Lady Almeda's fingerprints on the certificates were you to have them tested, Your Majesty."

"And the other, more serious matter of murder?" the king asked. "What proof do you have the Dearbhorgaills are responsible for the murder of their son?"

Eva glanced at Saber. The air around him started to sparkle, and an instant later, he stood before the king.

Naked.

Eva slid a quick glance at the king, saw his lips twitch once before his gaze went upward and fastened on Saber's face.

Unfazed by his nakedness, Saber took the bag from around his neck and removed several sheets of paper. "My name is Saber Mitchell, Your Majesty. I come from Middlemarch Resort on the planet of Tiraq, and I'm a friend of Eva's. This morning, I interviewed Huw Yolland and took his signed and witnessed statement. Lord Dearbhorgaill employed him to assassinate his son, Pryce."

"He confessed to the crime?" the king asked.

Saber nodded. "The Dearbhorgaills forced him to murder their son. Huw's wife and young son both worked in the kitchens at the Dearbhorgaill residence. The lord and lady incarcerated his wife and son in a dungeon on the lower floors of their residence and only released them after the deed was completed."

Lady Almeda gasped at her husband. "Fool! You told me you'd settled that *problem*."

"Quiet," Lord Loeiz snapped.

"I will read the statements," the king said.

"I'm not listening to this slander." Lord Loeiz wheeled around and headed to the door. Lady Almeda fell in behind, her long skirts rustling in an agitated manner.

"Hold," the king ordered. "Turlow, summon the guards."

"This is ridiculous!" Lord Loeiz shouted. "It's trickery! This woman tricked my son, stole his businesses, and now she wants to claim our currency for herself."

"The matter will be investigated," the king said.

"Rumor on the street says the Dearbhorgaills are in debt," Saber said. "They murdered their son to get their hands on his wealth, but he left everything to his widow. This created a problem."

"I see." The king's voice was hard. Angry.

Eva edged nearer to Saber, ready to intercede should the king decide to take action against him for some reason.

"You knew this? Suspected this?" The king fired the questions at Eva.

"I went to the authorities. They dismissed my concerns and told me I was hysterical."

"You had a legal marriage with Pryce?"

"Yes." Eva glared at the king.

"Turlow, take this information and start a royal investigation."

"Yes, your majesty," Turlow said. "And the Dearbhorgaills?"

"Hold them under house arrest until the investigation is completed. I expect this matter to be settled by tomorrow."

The couple shouted their outrage as guards escorted them from the chamber.

The king turned to Saber. "I can give you some clothes," he said with a slight grin.

"That would be excellent," Saber said.

The king cocked his head. "Where do you come from again?"

"My family lives on Tiraq, but we were originally from Earth."

"Where on Earth?" the king asked.

"New Zealand," Saber replied.

"That's where my brother lives. Prince Alexandre," the king mused. "Have you met him? He lives there with his wife, Lily."

Eva glanced at Saber, who shook his head.

"No, Your Majesty."

"No mind," the king said. "They come to visit fairly often. I'll send word when next they come, and maybe we could journey to your resort. I'll tell Turlow to make a note. Turlow will also summon you to court tomorrow once this matter is settled." And with that, the king rose from his throne and enjoyed a mighty stretch. "I'll have someone bring you clothes and show you out."

A short time later, Saber now dressed, they were escorted from the palace.

"The king intends to visit your resort," Robbie said, clearly awestruck, large eyes blinking from beneath the jagged hank of hair that flopped over his face. "Once that becomes known, your success will be ensured."

Saber wrapped his arm around Eva's waist and said, "He seems a fair ruler."

"He's known for being just. I wish I'd thought of seeking an audience before," Eva replied.

"You didn't have enough proof," Robbie said. "They can't refute the charges against them now. The king must agree otherwise he wouldn't have placed them under house arrest."

Saber growled at the back of his throat, and wide-eyed Robbie sprang away until a foot separated them. His cane dropped to the floor, and he clumsily stooped to pick it up. "Did you know he could do that?"

"Do what?" Eva asked, yawning.

"That...that cat thing," Robbie said.

"Yes. Don't worry. He won't hurt you. He's a pussycat."

"Meow," Saber said, and Eva started laughing. She didn't stop for a long time.

CHAPTER THIRTEEN

E va spent the next few hours at the original market restaurant, preparing for opening the following day. She mended broken shelves, scrubbed the kitchen from top to bottom, and bought fresh fruit and other supplies. Saber followed as bodyguard and helper. She devoted the rest of the afternoon and early evening to making sauces and stocks for the following day.

Her work ethic was incredible, impressing Saber and creating a sense of pride. As he pitched in, he found himself smiling and enjoying seeing this part of her.

His mate.

Pleasure suffused him at the thought. He'd never felt this level of emotion with Lori. He'd loved her, respected her. They'd been compatible in bed, but not to the same extent as him and Eva.

"Where have you gone?" Eva asked, poking him in the ribs.

He felt a silly grin form on his lips and couldn't stop himself from reaching for her hand and entwining their fingers. "I was thinking about Lori."

A frown creased her forehead for a nanosecond before she smoothed out her reaction, but Saber saw. Understood.

"No, not like that. I was thinking that you're more important to me."

"Oh," she said, still not looking at him.

She didn't understand the depths of his feelings for her, but he had plenty of time to prove himself. Still, might as well start reinforcing his groundwork. He didn't intend to leave her on Dalcon. She *would* return to Middlemarch Resort with him.

"What do you intend to do with the restaurants?"

Eva didn't hesitate, which told him she'd thought about her future, maybe their future and the thought pleased him. "I'm going to sell them. The new one—I might keep that until I can sell it as a going concern."

Saber nodded. "Good plan." He checked his timepiece. "It's getting late. You need some rest."

"I wanted to finish the prep for tomorrow."

"I'll help you in the morning. It can wait," Saber said, and tugged her to the door. He flicked off the lights, locked the door and pocketed the key. He took her arm and it trembled slightly as he led her out into the dimly lit alley. Surely she wasn't frightened of him?

Outside, the market bustled with activity. Ladies of various species offered their wares, a gambling den lured in punters with offers of quick riches, and the scent of roast meat wafted through the air.

"Hey, Eva!" A beefy man gave a cheery wave.

Eva started at the shout, although she returned the greeting. When another man hailed her, and she jumped again, Saber started to add the clues together.

"Eva—did someone harm you?"

She flinched again but didn't say anything.

"The Dearbhorgaills?"

"I think so. The attacker was interrupted before anything happened."

A woman shouted out and waved, and Eva returned the acknowledgment.

"Fuck," Saber snapped. "We must've scared you silly when we snatched you from your room."

Her chin lifted. "I bit your brother, and in the jungle, I kicked Bone Nose in the groin."

"You did a good job, kitten."

"Why did you snatch me like that, anyway?"

Hell. Now wasn't the time to fess up. "We like to give some women a real capture experience. It *is* written in the small print of the application form that a special capture is a possibility."

"But why, when you have all the different rooms and fantasy experiences? I don't understand."

Yeah, explain that, Saber. They'd reached the outskirts of the market area, where the buildings bore a coat of respectability. The doors sported bright, welcoming colors, and the windows sparkled during the solar day. Now, they glinted with muted welcome, the businesses still open doing a steady trade.

The hair at the back of his neck prickled without warning, foreboding roaring through his gut. "Eva..." His hand tightened on Eva's forearm and he drew her close, eyes scanning the groups of people, the dark corners. If there was danger, he couldn't see where the threat was coming from.

"What is it?" she whispered, traces of fear threading into her voice.

Saber cocked his head, sniffed the air. "I don't know." His gaze raked the shadows where illumination from the street lamps didn't reach.

A shot fired, the harsh bark of sound booming through an alley.

"This way," Saber ordered, a burst of fury pulsing through his veins. Fuckin' Dearbhorgaills. It had to be them. Nothing else made sense. Market people loved Eva. None of them would endanger her life. He wrapped his arm around Eva's shoulders and hustled her away from the direction of the weapon fire.

A second shot boomed. Much closer. Eva bucked against his chest, cried out. Saber smelled the blood, and fear weakened his knees. He staggered, regained his balance. "Eva!"

Eva had gone limp, and the scent of coppery blood filled his nostrils. His animalistic shriek of fury rang out. His cry resounded as he dragged Eva to shelter, heart pounding. He heard the thud of retreating footsteps, then only harsh breathing. His.

"Where are you hit?" His hands ran up and down her body.

"Arm hurts."

Illumination flooded the street.

"What is it? Who's there?" a timid feminine voice called out.

"Call the security force. Someone shot my mate," Saber replied in a harsh voice. "Where, Eva? Let me see."

"Hurts."

"I know, kitten." His voice was gentle despite the fear pulsing against his skin. His feline struggled for freedom, for the need to chase after the coward and exact revenge.

Maim.

Punish.

Mate!

"Let me see, kitten." He peeled away her fingers, which where clamped down on her upper arm, and surveyed the wound. Still bleeding, but it looked as if the weapon charge had grazed rather than penetrated. "It's gonna be all right," he crooned. "It's just a scratch."

"Hurts."

"I've called security," the woman called, her demeanor more confident now. "Can I help?"

"I need cloth, something to stop the bleeding." He hauled Eva farther into light and their helper gasped. Blood trickled down Eva's arm, seeped into her clothing. Saber saw her face was paler than usual.

"Am I gonna die?"

"No, kitten. Not tonight."

Maim.

Punish.

Mate!

His feline continued to buck beneath his skin and a growl leaked out, harsh and menacing.

The woman returned with cloth as a security vehicle purred through the air and settled on the street.

"I'll tend to her," the woman said. "You talk to security."

Saber was loath to release her, had to force himself to shift aside and let the woman with her cloth and bowl of water tend Eva.

"What happened?" a lean man in a black security uniform asked. The badge on his sleeve indicated his captain status, and his no-nonsense manner and the way he surveyed the scene told of his expertise. An underling stood at his side, silent apart from the tap of fingers on a genic tab as he recorded the scene.

"Someone shot at us. The charge hit my mate."

"Did you see them?"

"No. They kept to the shadows over there. They ran in that direction and took the lane to the left," Saber said.

The captain's eyes narrowed beneath the peak of his hat. "How do you know if you didn't see them?"

"I heard them," Saber said. "I have a dual nature. My other form is feline." He growled, unable to restrain his anger. "I'll catch them soon enough once I follow the scent trail."

"We'll check it out."

"I will aid your search once I settle my mate safely at home." Saber's tone brooked no refusal. He intended to catch this coward with or without their help. "This afternoon we had an audience with the king. I suspect the family we accused of a crime is attempting to subvert justice by killing my mate. She's been attacked in the market before. Someone means her harm."

The captain nodded slowly. "We'll wait for you. Wouldn't want to trample over the trail."

Saber nodded, appreciating a man who assimilated facts in a swift manner.

"We'll escort you home and wait while you settle your mate. Does she require medical care?"

"No. The charge nicked her arm. She will recover."

Saber thanked the woman for tending Eva and scooped up his mate, carrying her to the security vehicle. A short time later, they arrived at Eva's home, and he carried her inside.

"Help yourselves to a drink," he told the captain and his underling and hustled Eva up the stairs to her bedroom.

In the bedroom, he unwound the hasty bandage the woman had tied around Eva's arm. "The bleeding has stopped," he said, relieved to see the rough edges were already knitting together. Everything he remembered about mates seemed to be true.

Maim.

Punish.

Mate!

Saber subdued his feline with difficulty, batting him down with a cranky inward snarl. "Do you have painkillers? They'll help you sleep while I follow the trail with the captain."

"There's a bottle in the drawer over there. Do you think the Dearbhorgaills arranged this?"

"I'm sure of it," Saber said, rising to get the bottle and a glass of water. "They'll have several men on hire to do their dirty work. We'll get proof. Don't worry." He handed her two tabs and the water and placed a kiss on her temple. "Do you need anything else before I go?"

"No. Saber?"

"Yes, kitten?"

"Come back safe."

"I promise," he said, unable to resist kissing her lips. He forced himself to keep the kiss slow and easy, even though his feline squirmed beneath his skin, subtly demanding he imprint them both on their mate with a hard kiss and lusty sex. Saber fought the inner battle and forced himself to step away. "Sleep well, kitten."

The trail was simple to follow, and Saber made short work of leading the captain to the culprit. The skinny man—hell, he was a kid—strutted around a dim and dingy pub on the edges of the market. His eyes were alive with bloodlust, the excitement of taking another life, unaware he'd failed.

Maim.

Punish.

Mate!

Saber cut through the darkness in feline form, almost on the kid, before anyone noticed. When the kid saw him, he backed up, but Saber kept coming.

"Get away from me!" he cried out.

Not so cocky now. Saber snarled in the kid's face, displayed his sharp canines. *All the better to rip you limb from limb.*

"Back off. Leave him to us." The captain pushed past Saber and grasped the kid by his skinny biceps.

Saber snarled, the human part of him recognizing he needed to let this kid live. He gave the captain space and shifted to human.

The other patrons of the pub gasped at his transformation. A few commented about his nakedness. Saber didn't give a fuck. "Who paid you to kill my mate?"

"Don't know what ya talking 'bout," the kid said.

"Where were you an hour ago?" the captain demanded.

"I be here."

"Lie," Saber snapped. "I can smell it on him."

"You ask *them*." The kid jerked his thumb at the other customers.

Saber leaned closer, his nostrils flaring. "The weapon is in his pocket."

Panic flared in the kid's eyes. "Get your hands off me! I got rights, I do."

"Empty your pockets," the captain ordered.

"I got rights!"

"Who hired you?" Saber demanded.

"Let me handle this," the captain snapped.

"Fuck," Saber muttered and shifted back to cat. By the time he sat on his haunches in front of the kid, half the pub had cleared of customers. He kept his gaze on the kid, his mouth open and his sharp canines on display.

"Who hired you?" the captain asked as he confiscated the weapon.

"Some hoity servant," the kid said.

Saber growled.

"Said he'd pay me if I offed the woman."

"Would you recognize him again?" the captain asked.

The kid gave an emphatic nod. "I have to meet him tomorrow. Get the rest of my fee."

"Very well," the captain said, and turned to his underling. "Restrain him. We'll get his statement at the tower."

Saber transformed again. "We need to learn the servant's identity, determine if he works for the Dearbhorgaills."

"Tell me about the audience with the king."

Saber ran through the series of events while they waited for their transport to arrive.

The captain nodded. "And if you prove the Dearbhorgaills were behind this too, they'll be sent to prison."

The security transport appeared and settled on the road outside the pub. Two underlings secured the kid while the captain handed Saber his clothes.

Saber donned them rapidly.

"We'll arrange for the kid to make the meet tomorrow and identify the servant. I'll send word. If you've already left for the palace, I'll make sure I'm there myself to give a verbal statement."

"Thank you," Saber said.

"If you're interested in a job, I have one with your name on it," the captain said.

"Thanks, but I live on Tiraq. Have a business there with my family."

"Offer's there if you ever return to Dalcon," the captain said easily and shook Saber's hand.

He saw them off before heading to Eva's home, pleased with his night's work. The Dearbhorgaills would rue the moment they'd decided to go after Eva.

He'd make sure of it.

Eva woke with Saber curled around her, warm and solid. She hadn't heard him return.

"You're awake," he said, tugging a lock of her hair, a hint of mischief dancing in his eyes.

"Did you get him?"

"We did." Satisfaction coated his tone. "A servant hired him to do the job. The captain and I are confident we can tie him to the Dearbhorgaills."

"Good."

"How is your arm?"

She flexed it, braced for jagged pain—and felt nothing. "It's fine," she said in surprise. She sat up and unfastened the bandage covering the wound. She blinked. Instead of the angry wound she'd expected, the skin had knit together, the wound of the previous night reduced to tight pink skin. "It's almost healed! I don't understand." She turned to Saber. "How?"

He drew her into his arms and ran his fingers over her hair. "Remember when I bit your neck, and this cat tattoo appeared?" His finger drifted down to press against the spot.

"Yes." Eva gasped at the pleasure generated by his touch.

"Enzymes from my bite have entered your bloodstream. I need to consult with my mother, but I'm pretty sure that's why you've healed so well. You're my mate, Eva."

"Because you bit me?"

"Because my feline and I both wanted you—recognized you."

"I don't understand."

"We'll talk as soon as we've dealt with the Dearbhorgaills."

Eva's new com-circle buzzed, and she scrambled from the bed to pluck it off the nightstand. "Yes?"

"Ms. Henry, this is Turlow, the king's head courtier. His majesty will see you at noon when he intends to rule on your petition. I will notify the guards at the palace gate."

"Should I bring my assistant with me?"

"Not unless you wish it. The king has already heard his testimony, but you may bring one person to stand at your side."

Someone for moral support. "Thank you."

"Noon, Ms. Henry. Do not be late."

Saber escorted her into the palace a few minutes prior to noon.

Eva had chosen her clothing carefully, dressing in a light blue gown that molded to her body and made her feel confident.

A young courtier led them to a different part of the palace, where Turlow waited for them.

"Good. You're here," he said. "This way."

Eva and Saber entered the chamber after Turlow. This one was plainer, with white walls and white tiles on the floor. While the space was large, there were no windows in this room.

Several male clerks dressed in black robes sat at desks, with genic tabs and other administration equipment sitting in front of them. Beyond them, there was a seating area with not a spare seat to be seen, since they were all filled with lords and ladies—those from the elite Dalcon ruling class, the caste that was a step below royalty. There was a flurry of whispers as Eva entered the room. When Saber stalked in behind her, the whispers increased to a muted rush of excitement.

"Sit over there," Turlow instructed, gesturing at a row of chairs facing the audience.

"This is a travesty, I tell you." The piercing voice rippled into the room.

"Sounds as if your in-laws have arrived," Saber said in an undertone as the comments from those present became more audible.

"A disgrace."

"Unfounded accusations."

"Lies from a guttersnipe."

"Do you think they killed their son?"

Eva glanced at the Dearbhorgaills and saw they were dressed in their best clothes. Lord Loeiz wore a gray pinstripe suit cut to the trim lines of his body. His black shoes shone so brightly that Eva was certain a person would be able to use them for a looking glass. Jewels winked from the timepiece at his wrist, and a large blue stone the same cool blue as his eyes glinted from his left ear. Lady

Almeda wore bright orange, which contrasted with her long black hair styled in a complicated coronet on top of her head.

A somber man dressed in black stood at their side, a colorless spar-bird outclassed by two of the titled caste.

"Take your seats," Turlow ordered in a stern tone. "The king will arrive shortly."

Lord Loeiz drew himself up, contempt almost covering the faint tinge of embarrassment creeping into his cheeks. "She's a liar and a cheat. I don't know why the king is putting us through this travesty. It's clear she's jealous of our position in Dalcon society and wants to drag us through the same muck she inhabits."

"Still trying to use their position to cover their guilt," Saber whispered close to her ear. Eva caught his scent, a combination of wood, citrus and spices, as complicated as the man. Complex and exciting and very attractive. So sexy, and the things he did with her, *to* her...

He pulled away, shot her an amused, curious look that made her realize she was distracted. She couldn't afford to daydream. Not now.

"Hopefully the king thinks the same," Eva whispered back. Straightening, she pressed her spine against the back of her chair. At her side, Saber chuckled, and she found her own lips curving.

Footsteps sounded, and the men at the door straightened to attention. "All stand," Turlow intoned.

Everyone rose, and the king strode into the room, his official blue robes rustling with each step. He sat on his throne and surveyed the Dearbhorgaills, then her and Saber.

"All sit," Turlow ordered.

"Good, good. Everyone is here," the king said. "I have studied the documentation given to me yesterday, as well as the results of the court's thorough investigation. Before I inform you of my decision, is there anything you wish to add?"

"Yes," Lord Loeiz snarled. "This is all hearsay. The charges are unfounded."

"Not according to my investigation." The king's implacable tone set the audience whispering in excitement. "Everything appears as Ms. Henry stated. If anything, it seems her reports have been conservative in nature. Do you have anything to add, Ms. Henry?"

Saber gave her an encouraging nod, and she stood. "Last night an attempt was made on my life while we were walking home from my restaurant. The security force was able to capture the culprit and take his statement. Captain Jarvis has given me his com contact, should you wish to speak with him. He wanted to be here to give his report in person but has been called away on another case."

"Who was responsible?" the king asked.

"Lady Almeda Dearbhorgaill hired and paid the young male to shoot me," Eva said, letting her anger bleed into her tone. She winged disdain in their direction, her disgust at their duplicitous natures. They'd killed their son—not directly, but by association, and *frying fungus*, they were going to pay for their crimes.

"That's a wicked falsehood!" Lady Almeda cried, two spots of hectic color appearing on her cheeks at the open speculation from her peers in the audience.

Eva handed over the captain's written report to Turlow. "The report contains full details of the incident."

"You don't appear injured to me," Lord Loeiz said in a snooty voice. "Are you sure this isn't yet another fabrication designed to cast us in a bad light?"

Eva rolled up the long sleeve of her blue gown to reveal a white bandage around her arm, giving a theatrical wince. "It's still very painful. The captain of the security force was there. He saw the blood."

The king remained silent, but the lords and ladies seated in the room stirred and exchanged comments in undertones, the burst of sound resembling the passage of the wind through jungle trees.

"Quiet," Turlow roared.

The room fell silent, yet Eva's skin prickled from the bursts of curiosity, the greedy speculation.

"I will read this report," the king decided.

Eva ripped her gaze off the audience and strived to calm the bubble of nerves in her gut. It hit her, then, how things would go if the king decided for the Dearbhorgaills. Despite his earlier words, it could happen. Then she'd have nothing, no other recourse.

She'd have to leave Dalcon, start afresh.

Maybe she should do that anyway. Go with Saber...

But what of the future? Her future? Saber said they were mates. He hadn't looked at other women since they'd arrived on Dalcon, but that might change. Eva bore no illusions about her appearance. On a good day, she might attract attention from the opposite sex.

She wasn't sure she could face that—going with Saber and losing him to another woman. Losing Pryce had been bad enough, and they'd been more like friends. Saber...

Saber was different.

Even though they hadn't known each other long, she felt so much more for Saber. Something touched her thigh, and she glanced down to see Saber's hand. She curled her fingers with his, and her inner turmoil subsided.

It didn't matter what happened in the end. She was doing her best to right a wrong. If she failed today, she'd come up with another plan, and eventually, she'd prevail. Pryce's parents would go down and—

"I have come to a decision," the king said.

Murmurs filled the room again.

Turlow bristled and clapped his hands together. "Silence!"

Saber's fingers tightened around hers, and she gave him a stiff nod. She tried a smile, but it wobbled on her lips and wouldn't stick. She gave up and simply lifted her head to stare at the king.

"I have read the damning evidence presented to me by Ms. Henry—"

"She didn't even take the Dearbhorgaill name," Lord Loeiz snapped.

Lady Almeda sniffed. "She knew better."

The king ignored their outbursts and waved at Turlow when he would have shouted for silence. "Lord and Lady Dearbhorgaill have engaged in a series of vicious bullying tactics against Eva Henry. This state of affairs began when Ms. Henry became involved with Pryce Dearbhorgaill and has escalated since his death. I have signed proof from several sources—and the court's research provided the probable reason for this plot against Eva Henry."

The whispers and low comments grew louder as the king continued with his summation of the crimes and their possible causes.

"They did that?"

"Shame on them!"

"I can't believe it. They're titled."

"It's all lies."

"Quiet in the room," Turlow said when the noise became too distracting for the king to continue. "I will eject anyone who breaks silence."

The king continued. "The Dearbhorgaills have lived beyond their means for some time and were dependent on Pryce Dearbhorgaill to support their lifestyle. This is fact supported by financial inquiry. I personally believe they grew greedy and wanted more of Pryce's money. They mistakenly surmised killing their son would net them his estate. But Pryce married Ms. Henry, and together, they built a successful empire. Lord and Lady Dearbhorgaills have become increasingly desperate for currency to meet their needs and after learning their son left everything to his wife upon his death, they've continued to undermine Ms. Henry at every turn in an attempt to see her businesses fail. Last night, they paid someone to kill her."

"Lies!" Lord Loeiz cried.

Eva noticed Lady Almeda didn't comment, but she caught the flicker of fear on the woman's face, followed by the loathing in the glare her mother-in-law sent her way.

"We loaned her money to purchase her third restaurant," Lord Loeiz shouted.

The king held up his hand to halt further speech, and Lord Loeiz's face went almost purple as he ground his teeth together. "You made it impossible for her to obtain a loan from any credible source and hid your involvement in the loan company from her until after she'd accepted the terms and started work on her restaurant. Ms. Henry, if you'd known the Dearbhorgaills were behind the loan, would you have accepted it?"

"No," Eva said without hesitation.

"That is what I thought." The king gave Pryce's parents a steely look. "Lord and Lady Dearbhorgaill, I sentence you on four counts—the murder of Pryce Dearbhorgaill, the attempted murder of Eva Henry, theft, and destruction of property. You are hereby sentenced to imprisonment for the term of twenty-five solar years."

"No!" Lord Loeiz leaped to his feet. "You can't do this. It's her!" He pointed a finger at Eva, his eyes blazing with scorn. "She's a nothing—a *nobody*!"

"And in addition, the loan given to Eva Henry will be negated. Ms. Henry shall keep the monies advanced to her without the need to pay them back as compensation for the trials she has faced due to the Dearbhorgaills," the king continued, unfazed by the interruption.

"No. No, they'll kill us!" Lady Almeda cried.

The audience erupted into loud chatter, and Eva could literally feel the malicious enjoyment at the Dearbhorgaills' predicament.

"My sentence is final," the king said in a flat voice. "I will not sanction this type of crime in my kingdom, the abuse of power against those from lower castes. Turlow, take them away."

"No!" Lady Almeda shot to her feet and fumbled with her hair. Her locks toppled down around her shoulders in a dark curtain—and she plucked out a weapon, pointing it at Eva.

Eva stared, a hand flying to her chest. She willed her legs to move yet they refused to run.

"Conniving guttersnipe!" Lady Almeda screamed, her face twisted into a grotesque mask. Her hand held steady as she squeezed the trigger.

CHAPTER FOURTEEN

The weapon barked. Saber leaped at Eva and sent her flying to the floor.

Several women screamed. Men shouted. There was a stampede for the door. Turlow yelled for security.

Lady Almeda let out an annoyed screech and fired again.

"Keep your head down," Saber ordered, his voice close to her ear, his body a heavy weight across her back. Then his bulk was gone. A feline scream of rage rippled through the air. It built higher and higher until her ears hurt.

"Get away from me!" Lady Almeda shrieked.

A third shot discharged. Explosive. Deafening.

Eva saw Saber dive at the king and knock him off his feet. Another shot fired. Saber roared.

Security men rushed through the doorway. "Put your weapon down! Put the weapon down *now*."

They spread out, circling Lady Almeda.

"*Put your weapon down!*"

She ignored their demands and fired yet again.

Return shots fired.

A security man went down.

Lady Almeda crashed to the floor.

"Back against the wall," a security man barked at the remaining people.

Eva lifted her head. Despite orders to remain in place, she crawled across the tiles to Saber. The king was leaning over him. Blood squeezed between his fingers. Saber's blood.

The king glanced up, tears in his eyes. "He saved my life."

"Saber!" Her voice was hoarse, her heartbeat racing until it felt as if her chest would explode. He'd saved her too. "Saber," she croaked. She stroked his pale face and wished his eyes were open so she could see his pretty green gaze.

He couldn't die.

"Don't die, Saber. I won't let you. I refuse." *Frying fungus*, she loved him. She loved Saber with everything she had, and now it was too late to tell him.

"Hands up. Get away from the king," a security man boomed.

"Call the medical team," the king roared.

"Hands in the air!" the security man shouted, his voice edging into agitated. A weapon poked into Eva's ribs.

"It's all right," the king snapped. "It's not my blood."

Eva ignored the security team and lowered her head to brush a kiss on Saber's brow. A tear trickled down her cheek and dropped onto his nose. His nose twitched.

"He's going to be all right," the king whispered.

"Your majesty?" Turlow asked.

The king surveyed the swarm of panicked men and women and scowled. "Clear this room. Take Lord Loeiz to the jail. Remove Lady Almeda's body. Don't let anyone back in except the medical team."

"Yes, Your Majesty," Turlow said with a half-bow, turning away to issue orders.

"Saber," Eva said. "Saber?"

Saber's eyelashes flickered.

"See, I told you," the king said.

A medical man rushed into the room and sank down beside them, his white robe flowing around his spindly legs. "Let me look, Your Majesty," he said in a calm voice.

The king backed up until he sat beside Eva. He wrapped a comforting arm around her shoulders. "It's going to be all right," he repeated. "Saber is dual-natured. That makes him tougher than most."

As if to prove it, Saber's eyelashes flickered again. His eyes opened.

"Saber!" Eva said, some of her inner panic subsiding.

"Eva?" His voice sounded rusty and unlike him, but her relief was instantaneous.

"I'm here," she said, reaching for his hand. "I'm here."

While they'd been talking, the medical man had cut away Saber's clothing, baring the wound on his chest. He rifled through his medical bag and pulled out a sterilizing pad. He applied it to the wound and cleared away the blood.

Saber started to struggle.

"Hold him down," the medical man snapped.

"Saber." Her grip tightened. "You need to keep still, love."

"Need to shift," he gritted out. "Will help..."

"Release him," the king ordered instantly. "Step back."

The medical man's head jerked up in protest. "Your Majesty, I need to treat this man to stop infection."

"Step back," the king barked again.

The medical man huffed, his thin face full of disapproval, but he obeyed the king and moved away from Saber.

"Help me to my feet. Off with my clothes," Saber said.

His wound started to bleed again, and Eva bit her lip, worry and concern pressing against her chest. This couldn't be a good idea. "Saber, maybe you should let the medical man treat you."

"Need to shift. Help," Saber muttered.

Despite her misgivings, she and the king helped Saber to stand, then Eva used the medical man's scalpel to cut off Saber's clothes.

"Can you stand by yourself?" the king asked.

"Yes." Saber wobbled the second they released him, giving lie to his assertion.

"This is very irregular," the medical man said in a pompous tone.

Eva and the king ignored him, both focused on Saber as he lurched from side to side, his eyes tightly closed as he focusing on remaining upright. A faint shimmer glowed around his body. But nothing happened. Saber's face was pale and blood continued to drip down his chest and onto the tiles. Eva ached to go to him, but instead, she remained in place, shivering and biting her lip to hold back her anguish.

Then finally, *finally* the glow around Saber's body intensified.

Eva was used to him transforming quickly, but this time, it took long minutes. The clock in the corner of the room counted off the seconds until Eva wanted to scream. Saber's features began to twist, and the medical man jumped closer to examine his charge.

"Hold," the king ordered in a stern tone.

"But your majesty—"

Fur started to sprout on Saber's body, and he fell on all fours, a pained sound forging up his throat and emerging as a guttural groan. Saber cried out, but the shift continued, and eventually, a black leopard stood before them.

"Amazing!" the medical man said, awe shimmering on his face now. He edged nearer, his hand reaching out to touch Saber.

The king glared. "Move back. Don't touch him."

Eva crouched beside Saber and brushed her hand over his

shoulder. "Saber?"

Saber gave a tired sigh and leaned against her.

"How is his chest?" the king asked.

Eva ran a gentle hand over Saber's body. "It's stopped bleeding."

"Amazing," the medical man said. "I didn't know such a thing was possible."

"He needs to rest," Eva said. "Saber will require meat. He needs to rebuild his strength."

"You can stay here at the palace," the king said. "Turlow, organize two rooms for our guests. Adjoining rooms, please. Arrange for a meal and clothing. Take some from my wardrobe."

"Yes, Your Majesty," Turlow said and hurried off to carry out the king's bidding.

Soon, Eva and Saber were ensconced in luxurious rooms in the palace. Saber curled up on a soft sleep-bed, his eyes closed. Eva wasn't sure what to do to help him, but she figured sleep couldn't hurt.

A soft knock came at the door, and Eva hurried to answer the summons before the visitor woke Saber.

One servant waited with food and another with a selection of clothes. Eva opened the door wider and let them inside.

"Thank you," she said. "We'll serve ourselves."

The servants gawked at the black leopard curled up on the bed and hurriedly withdrew.

A grunt came from the sleep-bed, and Eva rushed over to see Saber was awake. She ran her hands over his fur. "Are you all right?"

He grunted again and slipped off the bed. There was a brief shimmer, and Saber transformed.

Eva rushed to his side and slipped an arm around his waist. The wound on his chest was a raw red color, but the edges of the wound had melded back together.

"You called me *love*." His voice was raw with emotion, the sentiment echoed in his green eyes.

"I...I...you saved my life. She intended to kill me. If it weren't for you, I would've died."

Saber lifted her chin with his fingertips and forced her to look at him. "I love you, Eva. I want to share my life with you, sleep with you, keep you safe. I want to spend my life making you happy."

A spark of warmth ignited in her, the seeds of which she'd kept hidden away in a locked box, safe and concealed, so she wouldn't get hurt. The yearning for love, for acceptance...Saber gave her that, she realized. He'd offered her a restaurant at the resort, the freedom to do what she did best. Cook and feed people. Make her customers happy.

This relationship was different from the one with Pryce. It excited her and made her feel giddy when she thought of the possibilities.

"Face it, Eva." His eyes pierced her with an emotional intensity. "I've captured you, and I don't intend to let you go."

Eva felt a slow smile spreading across her face. It became a grin of joy and spread so wide it hurt her lips. "And now that you've captured me, my love, what do you intend to do with me?"

"Love you," he said without hesitation. "Live with you. Have children. Be happy."

"Ch-children?"

"Yes." He had his bossy face on, and she found it rather endearing. "You can still work, do whatever you want, as long as it is at the resort with me. There are plenty of family members who'd love to babysit whenever necessary."

"My past...I don't know if I'd make a good parent." But she let herself imagine a small boy with Saber's beautiful green eyes.

"You *will* make a good parent, Eva. You would never abandon your child. You look after Robbie, your other employees. Bluebird. Me. Kitten, you have so much love in that heart of yours. You just haven't realized it yet. What do you say? Come home with me. Make Middlemarch your home."

Her breath caught, emotion swelling inside her until she didn't think she could contain the wealth of happiness.

"Yes," she said. "Yes." She smiled, and it was a little misty. "I might need to travel back and forth until the restaurants are sold, and I'd want to offer Robbie a job if he would like one at the resort."

"No problem." He eased back onto the sleep-bed, wincing at the pull on his wound where the skin remained tender.

"Are you all right?" Concern filled her at his pained expression.

"Need to eat," he said. "Refuel then sleep."

Eva scrambled off the sleep-bed and grabbed his meal for him. "Eat," she instructed before returning to eat her own meal on the small table.

"What happened to the Dearbhorgaills?"

"Lady Almeda is dead. Lord Loeiz is now languishing in the palace prison. I'm sorry on Pryce's behalf. Knowing his parents behaved in this manner would have caused him great pain. He was a good man," Eva said.

Saber growled around a mouthful of rare steak, and she grinned.

"They won't bother us again," she said.

"Good. Now I can get back to the normal headaches back at the resort," Saber said.

"Like what?"

"Someone keeps sabotaging the zylon fence and letting the wee beasties inside the resort compound. I have to manage the staff and stop the males from squabbling when they don't get a capture. I have to—"

"A capture?" Eva's eyes narrowed on Saber. She set her cutlery down to glare at him. "You arranged my kidnapping from the resort, didn't you?"

"Eva, that's not important now."

"It is to me," Eva said. "Tell me the truth. Now."

Saber's glance was cautious. "Just remember you're my mate.

My feline claimed you when I bit your neck. You wear his mark. He wants you, loves you. We both love you. Remember that."

"*Now*, Saber."

Saber scowled, then started talking. "I told you about the virus on Earth. It killed most of our females. We needed to find a way to attract women to the island and find mates for our people."

"Go on."

"We decided to offer capture fantasies at the resort. Most take place—*will* take place—within the resort, part of the vacation experiences we offer. But for some specially chosen women, my brothers and I intend to make the experience more...permanent."

"Permanent!" Eva sprang to her feet and advanced on him. "You had no intention of letting me return to Dalcon."

"No," Saber said baldly. "I wanted you, and I acted. You're our first official capture."

"I...you...but..." Eva took a deep breath, her mind spinning with his revelations. He'd wooed her, made such tender love to her, spanked her.

He'd saved her life.

That sloughed the abrasive edge off her thoughts. "You can't go around stealing women for your nefarious purposes." She poked him in the chest three times before she noticed his flinch of pain. "*Frying fungus!*" she muttered and backed up to glare at him. "What the hell am I meant to do with that information?"

"Love me," he said simply. "You know you want to."

The urge to laugh sneaked up on her, her merriment exploding into the room before she could control the inappropriate reaction. "I don't know whether to strangle you or kiss you in praise of your cheek."

"I vote for kissing."

Eva stared at him, her emotions in turmoil, but underneath it all, the truth kicked her in the gut.

He'd chosen her. He'd wanted her, and he'd set out to prove his desire and need for her. And with that truth, she melted. "Saber," she whispered.

"Come here, kitten."

Eva recognized the glint in his eye. "You're still injured. You need rest."

"I'll let you do most of the work."

Eva rolled her eyes but sank onto the edge of the sleep-bed and kissed him. The kiss started easy but morphed into hard and urgent. Her heartbeat soared at his taste, his desperate need for her, and the feel of his hands gripping her body, holding her close.

"Take off your clothes," he urged. "Please. I need you, kitten."

Seconds later, she slipped naked into his welcoming embrace.

"I love you," he whispered against her mouth.

"I love you too, you impossible man."

Their mouths slid together again, and their kiss was full of love and so sweet that tears formed in her eyes. The heat of arousal crept over her skin, and she writhed against him. His tongue stroked lazily into her mouth while his fingers skimmed across the tiny cat tattoo on her neck. Pleasure, hot and decadent, pulsed through her body, moistening her pussy and driving up the sensual tension.

"Saber," she moaned.

"I'm here, kitten. On top," he ordered in his next breath.

She laughed and kissed the tip of his nose. "Soon," she said and slid down the sleep-bed to straddle his legs. His cock thrust out, the head ruddy with arousal, and she ran her hands up and down his length, savoring the strength, the heat of his erection. Her fingers gently scored his balls, savoring the hardness of him, the quick way the tension ramped up in his body.

"You want me," she whispered.

"Always." His instant reply heated her as much as the arousal coalescing between her thighs. Her gaze went to his, connected and held.

"I want you too." Eyes still on him, she lowered her head,

watched his expression as her tongue lapped over his slit, cleared away the pre-cum that had gathered.

"You're beautiful. I can't look at you without wanting to fuck you. Even when I'm angry at you, pissed at you for running away and ending up in a cooking pot, I still want you beneath me, my cock shoved as deep as it can go."

Eva sighed, ran her tongue over the tip of his cock, and thought about him filling her as he described. His shaft bucked in her hand, pushed a little deeper into her mouth. His musky flavor danced over her taste buds. A twist of sensation converged in her pussy, and when she sucked on him, he made a purring sound of approval. The twist tightened, and she rubbed herself against his thigh, leaving traces of her juices.

"Enough," Saber growled. "Put me inside now."

Eva lifted her head, pulling off him with a popping sound. "Bossy," she muttered.

"*Eva.*"

Eva let her hair fall around her face to hide her grin and clambered into the position they both wanted. She guided his cock to her entrance and impaled herself. "*Ooh.* Feels so good when you fill me."

"Move," Saber ordered through gritted teeth. "Finger your clit and make yourself come."

"I hate to think what you'll be like when you're fit again." But she started rising and falling on his cock because it was what she wanted too. She rode him and rubbed her clit, gasping as pleasure spiraled out of control. Her sheath flexed around his cock and squeezed rhythmically when she started to come. She cried out, her eyes squeezing shut to savor the thrilling ride.

Saber gripped her hips and ground their bodies together, his harsh moan of animalistic pleasure setting off another series of ripples in her pussy.

Finally, they stilled, heartbeats slowing. Eva lifted off him and arranged herself at his side.

He pressed a kiss to her chin. "Love you, kitten."

She smiled at the burst of pleasure inside and wondered if the sense of awe would ever wear off. He'd picked *her* for his mate, wanted *her*.

Eva's smile grew as she pictured her life—*their* life. "You know, I'm not going to put up with you bossing me around."

Saber ran his hand over her head, his fingers coming to rest on her back. "So we fight, but we'll make love too, kitten. A lot. We'll laugh and maybe cry, face the odd crisis, but we'll be together. That's what life is all about."

Together.

Eva liked that a lot. And Saber was right. That's what life *should* be about. Two people together sharing everything. "I can't wait," she whispered.

"Me either, kitten. Me either."

They smiled at each other in perfect accord and sealed their love with another perfect kiss.

Get the Middlemarch Capture prequel (**Middlemarch Crisis**) for free by signing up for my newsletter (https://dl.bookfunnel.com/100tkhmmc2). You'll also learn about upcoming releases and receive free books, short stories tied to my series, and special promotion news.

Also, I want to ask for a favor. Word-of-mouth is crucial for an author to succeed. If you enjoyed this book, please consider leaving a review. Even if it's only a few lines, it would be a big help.

Please turn the page for a glimpse of *Favored by Felix*, book two in the Middlemarch Capture series.

EXCERPT – FAVORED BY FELIX

MIDDLEMARCH CAPTURE #2

C asey Seonaid wriggled and attempted to get comfortable. She flopped onto her side and prayed for the sweet oblivion of slumber. Seconds later, her body itched to move to a new position. *Scurvy sky pirates*, her brain buzzed like an angry drill-saw, too busy, too unsettled, too agitated to attempt sleep.

Finally giving up her valiant battle, she untwisted her body from the covers and slipped off her sleep-bed. She pulled on her robe—the garment she'd lovingly designed and made, rather than the complimentary resort one—and let herself out of the room she shared with her best friend, Eva Henry.

At this time of the morn, the Middlemarch Resort on the island of Ione, planet Tiraq, was quiet—too silent—and jerked her from holiday mode into military.

Just what she wanted to avoid.

Sighing, she held her body still while she went through the checks drummed into her by years of military training.

Look, watch, listen, smell.

Her glance proved she was alone. The long seconds she stood frozen confirmed nothing suspicious. Hearing check. Smell...

A slow smile curled over her lips. And she was back. The sweet fragrance of flowers, the close heat of the tropics, the faint tang from the waves running onto the shore scrubbed away the horrors of her job.

Automatically, Casey's feet turned in the direction of the sea. Bare feet, she realized, when she hit a gravel path. Too bad. She didn't intend to go back to their bungalow for something as pragmatic as footwear.

She limped over the gravel, another sigh gusting from her as she reached the more forgiving white sand. Her strides lengthened until she was almost running. As was usual, ever since her last meeting with General Seonaid.

Her father hadn't wanted a daughter.

He'd wanted sons.

Three sons.

And he sure as *phrull* didn't value her achievements or the way she'd advanced up the military ranks to match the careers of her two older brothers. No matter what she did, it wasn't sufficient.

She wasn't good enough for the general.

Casey slowed and padded across the white sand until she came to the edge of the water. A soft breeze wafted across her military-short hair and a wave washed over her feet. The water was cooler than she'd expected and startled a decidedly non-military *eep* from her throat.

"You shouldn't be out here alone," a male voice said.

Casey turned slowly, her leisurely action belying the way her heart drummed at her breast. Gods, she was more upset than she'd realized if someone could sneak up on her without raising her well-honed senses.

"Why not?" she asked and openly studied the big man who'd emerged from the shadows. "The resort is in a fenced compound. The place is full of women." Lousy with them, the general would say. The thought brought Casey great satisfaction. "What could happen to me here?"

The man walked—no, prowled was a better description for his gait—closer and came to a halt a few feet from her. He flashed a grin full of white teeth, and she found herself returning the expression. A natural smile instead of the conscious ones she forced for her best friend while she pretended everything in her world was perfect.

"Let me see." He pretended to ponder while his gaze slid over her in a way that made her feel like a woman instead of a soldier. "I've heard there is a race of aliens who have a shortage of women. They're out to steal themselves mates."

"I'm all a-shiver," she said, returning his gaze of interest.

There was much to be admired. His black hair hit his shoulders and was three—*phrull*—*four or five* times longer than her own black locks. Even in the dim light cast by the astral moon and the resort's artificial illumination, she could see his gorgeous green eyes. Just a few shades darker than the color of the jade sea that surrounded Ione. His broad shoulders were garbed in a loose white shirt, his lower half in tight black trews and black boots, and he was taller than her six feet by a few inches.

"And what if I'm one of these alien males?" His voice held a smoky tone that reminded her of late nights and smooth aged liquor on ice. He stood close enough now for her to feel the heat coming off his solid body.

"I should start running?" Gods, was that flirtation? She'd thought she'd forgotten how since one didn't fraternize romantically with fellow soldiers. She cocked her head a fraction. "Scream for help?"

"You're lucky, sweetheart. Tonight, all I'm after is a kiss."

And he grasped her shoulders and pulled her to him, his mouth covering hers in a hungry kiss before she could gasp out a protest.

Sensations struck her like laser fire. His hot mouth. His hard body. His expertise. The pleasure of contact ripped away her lethargy. She gasped, and he took advantage, sliding his tongue into her mouth and stroking against hers.

So nice. So good. So perfect.

Casey gripped his shoulders and let his mouth ravage hers, blast her with the sensations she'd craved for long, lonely months.

Finally, he lifted his head and grinned down at her while his thumb brushed across her tingling lips. "What's your name, sweetheart?"

"Casey."

"Felix," he said.

Her brows rose. "Not Alien Marauder?"

"Sexy Seducer."

Her brows inched a hairsbreadth higher, and she fought the burst of humor currently tickling her tongue for release. "You think you could seduce me?"

"Breathing elevated. Nipples hard. And if I were crass enough to check, I'd find you wet, or at least on the way there."

Common sense told her to knee him in the balls or punch his nose, but instead, amusement came to the fore, keeping the capable soldier at bay. "Rather sure of yourself, aren't you?"

"I haven't had any complaints." Those green eyes of his glittered in a silent dare.

"So are you going to capture me, tie me up, and keep me as your slave?" A shiver went through her at the idea of being his prisoner, and she knew he caught the tell because his grin amped up into a full-on smirk.

Phrull, she must be more tired and stressed than she'd thought.

"You like the idea," he whispered, his breath warm against her cheek.

"Not really," she said dismissively, while her mind screamed *liar*. Capture would solve her problems; put her out of reach of the general. *For a time.* He'd come for her eventually, though, and toss her right back into reality—and turmoil—until her loyalty was tested to the limits. Gods!

"Let me kiss you again," he said.

"You're asking this time?"

"I figured that way I could progress to touching your tits, check if they feel as beautiful as they look."

Casey forced back the hysterical laughter battling for release. Now wasn't that a kicker? One of the offending body parts that made the general hate her was the very part this sexy man wanted to touch. She shrugged, fought angry tears, and won. "Why not?"

Felix took her into his arms, pulled her tight to his body, and she discovered he wanted her. He liked what he saw. Heady stuff. She opened her mouth, let him use her as he wished, and drifted on the pleasure of his hands on her body, drifted on the knowledge he wanted her, just drifted...because it was safer than concentrating on reality.

Or her future.

Get Favored by Felix
https://shelleymunro.com/books/favored-by-felix/

ALSO BY SHELLEY

Middlemarch Shifters
My Scarlet Woman
My Younger Lover
My Peeping Tom
My Assassin
My Estranged Lover
My Feline Protector
My Determined Suitor
My Cat Burglar
My Stray Cat
My Second Chance
My Plan B
My Cat Nap
My Romantic Tangle
My Blue Lady
My Twin Trouble
My Precious Gift
My Grumpy Wolf

Middlemarch Gathering
My Highland Mate
My Highland Fling
My Elusive Mate
My Valiant Princess
My Highland Wedding
My Highland Billionaire

Middlemarch Capture
Snared by Saber
Favored by Felix
Lost with Leo
Spellbound with Sly
Journey with Joe
Star-Crossed with Scarlett

House of the Cat
Captured & Seduced
Claimed & Seduced
Merry & Seduced
Stranded & Seduced
Seized & Seduced
Hunted & Seduced
Festive & Seduced
Betrayed & Seduced
Enticed & Seduced

Dragon Investigators
Blue Moon Dragon
Blood Moon Dragon
Black Moon Dragon
Snow Moon Dragon

Dragon Isles
Liza
Cherry
Rena
Sasha

ABOUT SHELLEY

USA Today bestselling author Shelley Munro lives in Auckland, the City of Sails, with her husband and a cheeky Jack Russell/mystery breed dog.

Typical New Zealanders, Shelley and her husband left home for their big OE soon after they married (translation of New Zealand speak - big overseas experience). A twelve-month-long adventure lengthened to six years of roaming the world. Enduring memories include being almost sat on by a mountain gorilla in Rwanda, lazing on white sandy beaches in India, whale watching in Alaska, searching for leprechauns in Ireland, and dealing with ghosts in an English pub.

While travel is still a big attraction, these days Shelley is most likely found in front of her computer following another love - that of writing stories of contemporary and paranormal romance and adventure. Other interests include watching rugby (strictly for research purposes), cycling, playing croquet and the ukelele, and curling up with an enjoyable book.

Visit Shelley at her Website
https://shelleymunro.com

Join Shelley's Newsletter
https://shelleymunro.com/newsletter